What the critics are saying…

Love Slave

"…one erotic story you definitely won't want to miss!" ~ *Romance Reviews Today*

"…sweet and sensual, with a surprising depth in so short a piece." ~ *Simegen Reviews*

Forever Enslaved

"…a touching and poignant story of lovers who both want a happily ever after, but it doesn't come easy. Their journey is incredible and highly recommended! Don't miss it!" ~ *Road to Romance*

"Anyone looking for a stimulating love story about rebuilding a love connection will find Forever Enslaved to be an outstanding read." ~ *Just Erotic Romance Reviews*

Entrapped

"An elegantly written tale of two enemies who become lovers under the cruelest circumstances, "Entrapped" captures the desperation of these two scarred souls. It celebrates the beauty of love, which even chains and the possibility of death cannot destroy -- and the power of sex to heal the deepest of wounds. This story will arouse you and move you, often at the same moment. Another hot and painful gem by Ann Jacobs. ~ *Sensual Romance*

ANN JACOBS

SANDSTORMS

Ellora's Cave
Romantica Publishing

An Ellora's Cave Romantica Publication

www.ellorascave.com

Sandstorms

ISBN 1419954776
ALL RIGHTS RESERVED.
Sandstorms Copyright © 2006 Ann Jacobs
Edited by Sue-Ellen Gower
Cover art by Syneca
Forever Enslaved Copyright © 2005 Ann Jacobs
Love Slave Copyright © 2002 Ann Jacobs
Entrapped Copyright © 2003 Ann Jacobs

Trade paperback Publication March 2006

With the exception of quotes used in reviews, this book may not be reproduced or used in whole or in part by any means existing without written permission from the publisher, Ellora's Cave Publishing, Inc.® 1056 Home Avenue, Akron OH 44310-3502.

This book is a work of fiction and any resemblance to persons, living or dead, or places, events or locales is purely coincidental. The characters are productions of the authors' imagination and used fictitiously.

Warning:

The following material contains graphic sexual content meant for mature readers. *Sandstorms* has been rated E–rotic by a minimum of three independent reviewers.

Ellora's Cave Publishing offers three levels of Romantica™ reading entertainment: S (S-ensuous), E (E-rotic), and X (X-treme).

S-*ensuous* love scenes are explicit and leave nothing to the imagination.

E-*rotic* love scenes are explicit, leave nothing to the imagination, and are high in volume per the overall word count. In addition, some E-rated titles might contain fantasy material that some readers find objectionable, such as bondage, submission, same sex encounters, forced seductions, and so forth. E-rated titles are the most graphic titles we carry; it is common, for instance, for an author to use words such as "fucking", "cock", "pussy", and such within their work of literature.

X-*treme* titles differ from E-rated titles only in plot premise and storyline execution. Unlike E-rated titles, stories designated with the letter X tend to contain controversial subject matter not for the faint of heart.

Also by Author

৪৩

A Mutual Favor *(Also available in print)*

Awakenings

Black Gold: Another Love

Black Gold: Dallas Heat

Black Gold: Firestorm *(Also available in print)*

Black Gold: Zayed's Gift *(Found in the Mystic Visions anthology also available in print)*

Captured *(Anthology)*

Colors of Love

Colors of Magic

Dark Side of the Moon

Enchained *(Anthology)*

Gates of Hell

Gold Frankincense and Myrrh *(Anthology)*

Haunted

Lawyers in Love: Bittersweet Homecoming

Lawyers in Love: Gettin' It On

Lawyers in Love: In His Own Defense

Lords of Pleasure: He Calls Her Jasmine

Love Magic

Storm Warnings *(Anthology)*

Tip of the Iceberg

Books In Print
Lawyers in Love: The Defenders

Layers in Love: The Prosecutors

Contents

Love Slave

~11~

Forever Enslaved

~53~

Entrapped

~125~

~ Author's Note ~

Black Gold. The continuing story of two oil dynasties, of East and West coming together, of individuals not nations conquering age-old prejudice and forging partnerships based on love, the oldest of all human emotions.

Black Gold. A series that begins with a spoiled American coed persuading a hunky young Kuwaiti sheikh to fulfill her harem fantasy and continues over the period between the first Gulf War and the American invasion of Iraq. Seven contemporary erotic romances that celebrate the triumph of love against all odds…

Shana Green persuades Dahoud el Rashid to fulfill her fantasy…in "Love Slave." "Forever Enslaved" revisits the lovers ten years later, when the pressures of life have caused a rift that seems too deep to heal. "Entrapped" brings Dahoud's cousin Jamil home from years of imprisonment by the Iraqis. These are the stories in *Sandstorms*.

Firestorm, the story of Shana's brother Jake, slips chronologically between "Forever Enslaved" and "Entrapped". "Zayed's Gift" (found in the *Mystic Visions* anthology) concludes the series with the story of how Brian Shearer, a freed American prisoner of the Iraqis, finds happiness in Kuwait with Dahoud's younger sister.

There are two other books in the Black Gold series from Ellora's Cave, although the connection with the other five stories exists via secondary characters. *Another Love* takes place between "Forever Enslaved" and "Entrapped." *Dallas Heat* spins off from *Another Love.*

Ann Jacobs, award-winning author of more than thirty-five erotic romances, invites readers to visit her website, www.annjacobs.us to learn more about her and the books she has written.

Love Slave

৩

Prologue

She'd been bathed and waxed, perfumed and coiffed, draped in see-through gauze and gold and rubies. The harem master had taught her what to say in the sultan's exalted presence. A wizened eunuch escorted her along a pathway of pure gold, through a garden filled with fragrant and exotic specimens, to her lord's chambers. She bowed low, kept her gaze diverted, and prayed she'd please him so she'd be allowed to kneel at his feet and pleasure his magnificent cock.

Every day the fantasy intensified. Lasted longer.

The scene became clearer, the details more erotic. Shana Green's fantasy sheikh spirited her away from her ordinary college senior's world of books and dates and after-graduation plans and locked her away, his sex slave in the sybaritic luxury of the harem.

She couldn't stop seeing that other world in her mind, couldn't stop dreaming about a lifestyle totally foreign to everything she'd known.

She wouldn't give up the fantasy, sentence herself to a lifetime of boring missionary position sex and groping in the dark. Especially now.

Now her fantasy man had the face of a dark angel and a hard, muscular body that put most men's to shame. And a name. Dahoud el Rashid. Or "Bear," as he'd told her and her brother Jake his teammates called him.

It was as though she'd seen him in her mind and, poof, he had materialized out of thin air.

Shana laughed. To be perfectly accurate, fate had sent the sheikh pounding into her six-four, two hundred pound baby brother while Jake threw his first college game pass for the Longhorns' arch-rival Texas A&M last Saturday. And he'd dropped into her sights when he came by the hospital to make sure Jake was okay.

Amazing. That gorgeous male specimen had escaped her attention for the three plus years they'd both spent so far on the UT campus here in Austin, Texas.

Not really. Even a fantasy man could stay anonymous among forty thousand or so students.

It wasn't as if they moved in the same circles. Shana was the quintessential Jewish American princess, Bear a Kuwaiti foreign student who happened to be the Longhorn's star linebacker.

Well, the princess was about to escape the castle.

If all went according to plan, she'd soon live out the fantasy she'd spun in her head for years. Bear didn't know it yet, but he'd soon capture her and drag her off for a temporary stay in his harem.

Fate had practically tossed the sexy sheikh into her arms, and Shana was not a woman to ignore opportunity.

Stretching naked before a full-length mirror, she eyed herself critically.

Her legs were long and silky, waxed smooth a week ago when she'd had a Brazilian bikini wax. Her thighs were firm and slender, just right for locking around Bear's narrow waist.

Her pussy looked pale beside that neatly trimmed landing strip of curly dark brown hair. Duly noted. Pussy could use a few sessions in the tanning bed before being offered up to her sheikh's talented tongue.

Shana liked the impressive ruby belly-button ring she'd bought when her piercing finally healed. It had hurt like hell for months, which was why her only other piercings were the single ones in each ear.

Her boobs and ass had enough curves to entice her sheikh. Unless he had a thing for overblown and overweight. Nah. Not *her* fantasy man.

She tossed her dark hair over one shoulder, smiled at her reflection. Pretty ordinary, she decided. Not the stuff of sonnets, but she wouldn't scare kids on Halloween, either.

Decently long lashes accentuated eyes that weren't quite brown or green but something in between. She'd always wished they were one or the other, but the color was interesting. At least her nose looked good, thanks to Dr. Berger's skill. And Beth Levin's dad deserved the credit for her straight, white teeth. But the full lips boys had called kissable since sixth grade were all her own.

All in all, the package came together pretty well. And thanks to a rich, generous daddy and a mother who'd seen to it her daughters knew how to maximize their assets, Shana had all the tools she needed to enhance it.

She was about to grab some of those tools and go out hunting Bear.

Chapter One
Austin, Texas, May 10, 1990, six months later

ಬ

"You want what, my lord?"

Sheikh Dahoud al Rashid, "Bear" to his friends at UT, shifted the cell phone to his other ear. "A eunuch, a couple of *houris*, and enough close-mouthed servants to staff the harem at El Rashid. And I want them in place by tomorrow."

Asad al Qassimi, Bear's new assistant, hadn't balked when told to open up and prepare some rooms at the family's ancient fortress near *Mina Su'ud* overlooking the waters of the *Khalij*. He'd arranged for a family jet and crew to take his new employer and a friend from Austin to Kuwait City without raising an eyebrow.

Apparently Asad had a problem now.

"My lord. Your father—"

"My father does not need to know. See to it." Annoyed, Bear shut off the phone.

His mouth watered and his cock throbbed at the prospect of spending five days with the most beautiful, sexiest, and least suitable woman on earth.

Who'd have thought going to check on the Aggies' freshman quarterback he'd knocked out would have brought him face-to-face with a woman who chased all the others from his mind? Or that his dream woman would want to sample life in a sheikh's harem and refuse to sample *him* any other way?

His business degree in hand since earlier today, Bear now had to take hold of his family's business. But before he did, he'd enjoy one last hurrah.

Shana Green would someday be only a fond memory. For the next five days he'd be creating those memories.

"Bear!" she called from across the quad.

He loved her spontaneity, her irreverent ways. Her balls, he would say in American slang if she were a man.

Now it was time for her to become his temporary *houri*.

Bear sprinted across the campus green, tossed Shana over his shoulder, and hauled her to a waiting limousine where he slipped a black silk pillowcase over her head.

* * * * *

When Bear removed the thing he'd tossed over her head, Shana looked around a room that seemed more like a luxury hotel room than a sheikh's bedchamber until the floor began to vibrate. They were on a plane. Obviously private and bigger than the Boeing 737 Daddy's company used to ferry crews to oil fields around the globe.

"Where are you taking me?" she asked over the roar of the jet engines.

"To El Rashid. My harem on the Arabian Sea. "

Bear looked fearsome in his desert robe and a *ghutra* that framed his hawk-like features. If this hadn't been an arranged capture, Shana would have been quaking with fear. Even so, the garb made him look dark, powerful. Foreign and inscrutable. And incredibly sexy.

Was Bear naked under his flowing robe?

Her mouth watered. She toed off her high-heeled sandals and popped the button loose that held her dress together at the waist. "Am I your captive?"

"You're my *houri*, here to bring me pleasure. You are not, however, very well trained. We have the next fifteen hours to work on that. Disrobe and kneel."

Her nipples hardened. The muscles in her lower belly clenched. Her mouth watered, and her pussy began to twitch. Bear wasn't a sweaty boy like the ones she'd experimented with before. He was her fantasy man.

He'd made her nipples pucker and her pussy perpetually ache since the day fate dumped him into her fantasy. Now she quaked like a virgin beneath his hawk-like stare, her fingers unsteady when she unfastened her bra.

His sensual lips curved in a sardonic smile. "Do you need assistance?"

"No."

"No, my lord." She caught the hint of amusement in his tone.

Shana dropped the bra at his feet. "This, too, my lord?" Hooking her thumbs into the sides of her thong bikinis, she shot him a playful grin.

He nodded, his gaze locked on the jewel in her belly button. "Do you dance?"

"I will dance for you, my lord. I've taken lessons," she added when she noticed his dubious expression.

Shana tossed her panties his way and dropped to her knees. "Do you want me to show —"

"Take off my shoes."

The hems of khaki slacks rested on highly polished loafers that seemed incongruous with the robe. She'd imagined finding bare, golden skin instead.

He lifted his feet so she could tug off the shoes. "Socks, too."

Shana stroked his large bare feet, enjoying the contrasting textures of the rough, callused soles and his smooth brown toes.

"Kiss them."

How did he know that's what she wanted to do? Lowering her head, she sucked his big toe into her mouth.

He must have washed up for this capture gig, because his feet actually smelled good, like sandalwood soap and fine English leather. She sampled another toe, tickling it with her tongue.

Her nipples tingled at the prospect of sampling him all over.

His cock would be big and smooth, and he would taste oh, so good when she took him in her mouth.

She sucked harder, tried to concentrate on the task he'd given her instead of fantasizing about his more interesting parts.

"Remove my slacks. Then you may lie back on the bed," he said, his voice gruff.

Good. No belt and no underwear. Her heart beat with eager anticipation when his pants were off and she lay back, legs spread, across the quilted coverlet.

Praise Allah! A sybaritic feast lay before his eyes, waiting to serve his pleasure.

Bear drew her toes into his mouth and sucked them one by one. He stroked his way up tanned, satiny calves, his lips following his hands.

Damn. The traditional headdress got in the way. He paused, tossed it and his robe away, and resumed a slow, sensual journey, lifting one of her legs and nibbling at the sensitive spot behind her knee.

Shana slid her legs farther apart, as though to give him better access. And when he moved his hand higher, she let out a sexy little moan.

God, she was responsive. And he loved her warm, wet *yoni,* satiny smooth to his touch but for the neatly trimmed, narrow strip of dark hair in the center of her suntanned mons.

His mouth watered. His cock throbbed. "Why not remove this, too?" he asked, fondling the patch of crisp pubic hair.

"You like pussies totally naked, my lord?"

"We remove all body hair."

"You mean your women do?" She lifted her hips, opened herself wider for his inspection.

"Men as well." He bent, licked her baby-soft outer lips. She tasted of almonds and hot, aroused woman, made him want to dispense with the role-playing and lose himself in her delectable flesh.

Her gaze dropped to the silk boxers that barely contained him. "You?"

"You've never seen a hairless cock and balls?" he asked, blowing on her clitoris and watching it swell and come erect.

"Not yet, but I'm hoping I will, soon. I want to taste them, too."

"If you're very good, I may let you." *For a split-second, perhaps, before I bury my cock in your sweet pussy. But after you take the edge off my hunger, you may devour me for hours if that is your wish.* Bear tongued her, sucking her clit into his mouth and nipping gently at it with his teeth. Her whimpers of pleasure urged him on.

Not in her wildest fantasies had Shana dreamed he'd drive her mindless with his tongue. No one had ever managed to do it before. She gasped when her pelvic muscles contracted and began to convulse.

"I want you inside me now."

He paused. "Come first and then I'll fuck you." Grasping her knees, he spread them wider apart and resumed his tender assault on her clit while he stroked the backs of her knees, his fingers making sensuous circling motions that—

"Ohhhh. Stop. I'm coming. Don't. Don't. Don't stop!" With both hands she held his head while he lapped the juices from her dripping pussy.

Shock waves still coursed through her when he lifted his dark head and stood, shoving down his underwear and revealing the hardest, most beautiful, and—she gulped—*biggest* cock she'd ever seen.

Her pussy clenched in the middle of a contraction.

His eyes scorched her with their stygian fire.

Impressive muscles bulged in his shoulders…his massive thighs…that purple-knobbed, rock-hard column of circumcised male flesh she wanted inside her now.

It stood straight up against his flat belly, its single eye glistening with a drop of fluid that beckoned Shana's tongue. She itched to fondle the deep-rose, velvety looking sac that held his big balls tight against his groin.

She didn't realize she'd moved until she found herself within licking distance of this fantastic lollipop that exceeded her wildest imaginings. So big. So clean looking without the usual tangle of male pubic hair.

Her tongue darted out and sampled him. Tasty. She opened her mouth, took him inside, and swirled her tongue over his satiny cock head. It took both her hands to cradle the incredibly soft-skinned pouch that held his heavy testicles.

"Cease." With both hands Bear lifted her head.

Shana looked up, saw a muscle twitch on the side of his jaw. Good. She'd make him lose that iron control.

He came down on top of her, flesh to flesh. With his powerful legs, he spread hers wide apart. His huge cock nudged her pussy, throbbing and making her incredibly horny. "Do you want this now?" he asked, his voice ragged.

She lifted her hips, took the tip of him inside. "Yes, please. Fuck me, my sheikh."

Chapter Two

೧೦

"My pleasure."

Her *yoni* gripped his unsheathed cock like a wet, hot fist. No condoms, she'd insisted before dragging him to her doctor two weeks ago for them to have the tests no sane person would have unprotected sex without, and extracting his promise to keep his cock out of strange pussies until now in exchange for hers that she'd stay on the Pill.

She squeezed him with her inner muscles, made him want to come. Made him want to stay in her forever, prolong the incredible sensation of fucking her hot, wet pussy without any barrier.

He withdrew, sank into her deeper, harder, took her orgasmic cries into his mouth when he changed angles and hit her G-spot.

He'd never had such a responsive lover. And he'd never spurted his semen deep into a woman's *yoni*. Never before had he itched to impregnate his partner, see her slender belly swell with his child.

He did now.

She milked his cock as though she wanted that too. He wouldn't last long.

But she'd shatter along with him.

Bracing himself on one elbow, he reached between them and massaged her clit.

She moaned into his mouth, sucked his tongue inside. Clenched her pussy onto his cock. Dug her nails into his shoulders and clutched him with her legs.

When she convulsed around him, shouting her pleasure, she triggered his shuddering climax.

It seemed to go on for hours. He thought he'd die with each powerful spurt that showered her pussy with his hot sperm.

Ten minutes later his cock was twitching, obviously hot to fuck her again.

* * * * *

By the time they landed in Kuwait City, they'd fucked and sucked and indulged in every act of pleasure Shana ever imagined. And then some.

Now her fantasies would come alive, for real.

The *abaya* he handed her tickled her sore, swollen nipples as it settled it against her naked body. She felt possessed. Captive.

"Like this, love," he said when she had trouble draping the silk *hijab* over her forehead. "Now the *shaila*."

The black veil felt heavy. Repressive. How could Arab women live like this? Bear's hand weighed heavily on her elbow when they crossed the tarmac to a waiting limousine.

They sped through a city that looked surprisingly modern. Men in western clothes, even a few bareheaded women, mingled with traditionally dressed natives along the busy streets. Bear must have chosen traditional garb to indulge her fantasy, not because it was required or even expected.

He acted anything but traditional in bed. Her pussy muscles clenched when she recalled what they'd done the past fifteen hours.

"The Iranians destroyed much of the ancient infrastructure when they bombed our oil installations in

1981," Bear explained after she commented that many of the buildings looked new.

He'd been thirteen years old then. "Those must have been scary times," she commented as the scenery began to change.

"I wasn't here to see the destruction. By then I was already in the States, in boarding school. Look to your right. That's one of the el Rashid well fields."

Sand and dust and oil wells stretched as far as Shana could see. It didn't look much different from the GreenTex fields in west Texas, where Jake worked every summer. When she told Bear, he laughed.

"If not for the issue of our different cultures, our families would be salivating at the thought of merging two oil dynasties," he said.

But that was a huge issue. Their parents would pitch fits if either of them brought the other home as a potential mate. After all, their ancestors had started the tradition of enmity long ago, and hatred had been passed down through too many generations for mere lovers to overcome.

She only wanted to experience her fantasy. To chase it and her sexy Arab sheikh out of her mind so she could get on with her life.

Shana tried to remember that when Bear closed the heavily tinted window that separated them from the driver.

When he lifted her onto his lap and impaled her on his hot, hard cock, she decided there was something to recommend these loose Arab robes.

Especially when lovers were naked underneath them.

She slipped her hands behind him, cupped the satin-smooth cheeks of his tight ass and ran her fingers down the dimpled cleft that separated them. His growl disappeared down her throat when he clamped his open mouth over hers and thrust his tongue inside.

His huge cock throbbed so deep inside her, she couldn't say where he ended and she began. She flexed her vaginal muscles when he started to lift her off, let them go slack seconds later when he brought her down on him while he flexed his hips and stuffed his entire length in her.

Wet, hot, velvet-covered orbs. That's what his testicles felt like against the outside of her pussy now that her own juices flowed around his cock, over his balls. So delicious. So arousing, the first waves of an incredible orgasm took her breath away.

"Come for me. Again and again. Milk me dry," he whispered against her mouth.

Delicious sensations centered between her legs. Her clit swelled where the base of his swollen cock and his clean-shaven pelvis stimulated the sensitive tissue each time he thrust deeper into her weeping pussy.

Then he nudged her *hijab* aside, grazed her neck with his teeth. His hot breath sent frisson of excitement to her breasts.

Her nipples beaded and hardened, seeking his mouth but finding only the heavy black fabric of the *abaya*. Her clit spasmed again.

Wave after wave of luscious sensation swept over her, through her, leaving her slumped against Bear's powerful body.

He seemed insatiable, nibbling her earlobes through the fine silk of the *hijab* while he fucked her faster, deeper, harder. Shana reached under his soft white robe again, tweaked his flat male nipples.

"Fuck me harder. Make me come."

He took her mouth after that anguished plea, while he grabbed her at the waist, lifted her, and slammed her down on his cock.

It felt as though he was sucking the breath out of her when he stiffened and shuddered with the power of his orgasm. Feeling his semen spurt deep in her pussy triggered the most powerful climax she'd ever experienced.

* * * * *

After a couple of hours, most of which they'd spent on a roller coaster of sexual arousal and satisfaction, they arrived at an ancient fortress set high on a hill overlooking the *Khalij*, as Bear called the Persian Gulf. Made of pale stone that blended into the sandy terrain, it rose suddenly in their path, as though it were an illusion.

Maybe it was. An illusion come to life, part of the fantasy that had brought Shana to Bear's home. His bed.

Some long-ago sheikh had built the villa around a walled courtyard paved with ancient-looking tiles whose bright colors had faded over the centuries to soft tones of blue and rose and sepia. Shana and Bear passed brambles of long-neglected rosebushes and towering date palms. Yellow blossoms that smelled like exotic perfume trailed along the marble that surrounded a sparkling fountain.

"The women's quarters await you. You will pleasure me tomorrow. I must make up to my other women for having neglected them these past months."

Jealousy gripped Shana, but she reminded herself this *was* her fantasy—to become a sheikh's *houri*, maybe even a *kadin*.

Of course that wouldn't happen. She wasn't going to swell up with Bear's child.

But for a few days she'd indulge that fantasy, pretend she wasn't on the Pill.

"My lady Shana?"

"Yes?" The slight, soft-spoken servant wore loose trousers gathered around his ankles and a vest that looked like a woman's multicolored bolero. He wore a matching turban.

Shana couldn't resist glancing at his feet, expecting to see fanciful curly-toed shoes out of an illustrated translation of *Ali Baba and the Forty Thieves*. Learning he had on beach thongs disappointed her.

"I am Selim, master of my lord's harem. If you would follow me..." He turned on his heel, obviously expecting her to come along.

Her eyes widened at the opulence of a large, sunny central room with potted plants and a steaming, sunken marble bathing pool. A voluptuous blonde lay naked on a couch beside the pool, where two other women—servants, Shana guessed by their simple robes—massaged her pale, ivory skin.

"That is Alexandria. The other one practicing the dance she will do for my lord Dahoud is Iris. Regrettably, having been at university in a country that frowns on our way of life, the sheikh has only them—and now you. I expect he will fill his harem again ere long."

Iris, a top-heavy redhead whose outfit looked like what Jeannie wore in the old TV show, *I Dream of Jeannie*, undulated to the sensuous rhythm another servant beat out on the *tabla*, a drum similar to the one Shana's belly-dancing instructor used.

No way would Shana share her few short days with Bear. She'd find some way to have her sheikh all to herself. Unless...

Unless she got herself invited to join in the fun. She got wet, imagining Iris dancing and the blonde running her tongue over Bear's gigantic cock while he took care of Shana's own dripping pussy with his mouth.

When had she quit thinking of him as her fantasy sheikh and started thinking of him by the nickname his teammates had given him?

She suspected it was about the time her pussy fell head over heels in love with his slick tongue. And his clean-shaven, enormous cock. That would have been the first time they made love, thirty thousand feet over some southeastern American farmland.

"My lady?" Selim looked nervous, as if he didn't know how to proceed. "May I help you disrobe?"

"I can manage." She grinned. Head-to-toe black looked out of place here, where it seemed the sheikh's women relaxed naked, or darn close to it. Still, she wasn't strictly comfy stripping down in front of a man, even Selim who seemed safely asexual—and that's exactly what she'd be doing if she took off the *abaya*, since she had nothing on under it.

"Would you mind finding me something to change into?"

Selim glided to an anteroom and gestured at the selection of garments. "May I select something that will please my lord?"

"Go ahead. Then leave. I'm not stripping down for your entertainment."

He selected a filmy rose-colored pants-and-bolero combo that looked as if her most interesting parts would be covered by pearl and crystal beadwork. Then he met her gaze. "Entertainment? My lady, I am a eunuch. Were I not, I could not enter the women's quarters and live."

They still cut off men's balls to provide guards for harems? Shana had thought that practice ended a century or more ago. "Tell me the sheikh did not order you—" she searched for the right word—"gelded."

"No. It is forbidden for a Muslim to unman another. Eunuchs are made by infidels."

Infidels. The Arabs' catchall word for all human beings who weren't Muslim.

The word for people like her.

What a strange society. Fabulous wealth from oil apparently had resulted in a dual sort of life for sheikhs like Bear, who seemed as at home in western dress playing American football and flirting with modern college women as he did here in his homeland where he accepted his right to keep his *houris* in this opulent prison called a harem. It was difficult to believe he could be oblivious to the pain men like Selim went through to provide protection for his property.

Of course, Shana thought as she stripped down and stepped into the steaming bath, there were inequities in all societies.

Why did she try to justify such barbarism? This was not a lifestyle she'd consider embracing. She'd known from the start, and so had Bear, that their relationship could go nowhere. He belonged here; she belonged in Houston.

She lay back, let the warm water swirl around her. A sweet, faintly musky fragrance rose in the mist, saturated her pores.

Roses? Shana didn't think so. The heavy, exotic scent fit the ancient women's quarters, made her think of the tales she'd devoured. She pictured hundreds of *houris* and their servants crowding every corner of this magical villa on the sea. Too bad for Bear there were only the two bimbos—and her, for the next three days—to see to his sheikh-ly pleasures.

Of course he only had one cock—the only cock the women he kept in his harem could ever hope to enjoy. Why did the idea of him having no variety not disturb her as much as the thought of sharing his big pleasure tool?

Idly, she bit into a fat stuffed date. The tartness of the iced, nonalcoholic fruit drink Selim gave her contrasted with the date's sticky sweetness.

Boob job, she thought uncharitably when Alexandria got up from her couch and slipped into harem pants and a matching bolero that didn't come close to covering her hennaed nipples. Nobody had tits that round, that big—without a plastic surgeon's help.

The woman probably had liposuction, too. Chiding herself for her small-minded thoughts, Shana stepped out of the tub.

Suddenly the sound of a gong split the silence. Selim clapped his dainty hands. "My lord sheikh summons the ladies Alexandria and Iris to his chambers. Come now, my pretties."

Shana clenched her fists, fought the rage that had built inside her, and whispered her own plan in Selim's ear. She might have to share her sheikh, but she'd not languish here alone while he had his fun.

She'd never in her life had a murderous thought.

But the idea of stuffing the bimbos into silken pillowcases and tossing them into the sea suddenly had great appeal.

* * * * *

The actors Asad had hired were obviously bored, but the women perked up when Selim explained the sex scenario Shana wanted to act out.

Lying naked on a towel-covered couch while two servants removed a week's growth of his body hair, Bear held up his hands. "Cease the discussion. You will act out the lady Shana's fantasy with me tonight." The fistful of *dinars* he planned to give them would hopefully keep word of this debauchery from reaching his mother's ears.

"I'd gladly share your couch," Iris said, her long nails tickling him when she traced a pattern down his freshly depilated chest to his cock and balls. "Alexandria and I can show you a good time. Better than the American."

Bear modified his impression. The women apparently were call girls, not actresses. Hookers as the guys in Texas called them. The blonde obviously enjoyed plying her trade.

"Do not forget me, my lord."

When the eunuch aimed a hungry gaze at Bear's groin, he got the uncomfortable feeling he was being sized up for a potential meal. "My appetites do not include eunuchs," he growled.

"I'm no eunuch."

Fury rose in Bear's chest, made him clench his fists. This man had looked on Shana's nude body. "Then what the hell are you?"

"An actor hired to play a eunuch. Oh, do not fear. I have no interest in women. Your lady is quite safe. Now, you, on the other hand…"

Bear squelched the sudden urge to snatch up a towel and cover his nakedness. If his temporary harem master was as gay as he acted, Shana should be safe. She qualified as one hundred percent delicious female.

Still…he didn't like the idea of another man looking at her.

Damn it, he'd told Asad to hire a eunuch.

He practically laughed out loud at his own stupidity. This was 1990. No more markets existed to purchase *houris* and eunuchs. Harems didn't exist, except in the most isolated and backward parts of the Muslim world.

Obviously Asad had found it difficult to re-create exactly a world that existed only in Shana's dreams. Bear's orders had been too daunting, even for his highly efficient assistant.

Bear had embraced Shana's fantasies because he wanted to embrace her. Somewhere between Austin and here, he'd decided he wanted her permanently, not just for a brief interlude.

With luck he'd play out that scenario tonight so he'd have two days left to sell her on the reality of loving him — and sharing his life.

"You two. Stay. You may show me the good times you promised — later." Bear turned to Selim. "Go back to the women's quarters. Wait an hour, then fetch the lady Shana. If you touch her, rest assured you will become a eunuch, in truth."

Selim laughed as he made a show of bowing his way out of Bear's presence.

Waving away the servants massaging fragrant oil into his skin, Bear turned to his temporary *houris* and told them what he wanted them to do.

Chapter Three

Shana wanted to kill the bimbos.

She wanted to kill Bear.

She wanted to crawl in a hole and die of embarrassment because her pussy dripped at the prospect of joining him and the others in a *ménage a trois*.

Not trois. There would be four of them.

What was four in French? Too bad she'd forgotten. If she hadn't, she'd be able to figure out what one called that.

Group sex?

Shana tittered nervously as she followed Selim through the courtyard. Muffled beats of the *tabla* wafted through the air, along with the reedy sounds of some other instrument.

Exotic sounds that made her want to dance for Bear. To ride his cock to pleasure.

"Enter."

Selim opened the door, bowed, then stepped aside.

An antique Persian rug felt warm against Shana's bare feet. Its jewel tones echoed those in tiles along all four walls. Opened double doors let in the light of the crescent moon that hung over the *Khalij*.

A gentle breeze ruffled Shana's hair, ballooned the diaphanous fabric of her harem pants and made her damp pussy pucker from the sudden chill. It made thousands of fragrant candles flicker, casting the huge chamber in shadow, then in soft, sensual light.

Smoke curled from a brass container. Incense. Sandalwood, with a touch of something exotic, erotic.

Her mouth went dry when she saw Bear, reclined in all his naked glory among dozens of colorful pillows on the biggest sleeping couch she ever saw. His satiny olive skin glowed. Every tiny movement of his massive chest muscles when he breathed tempted her to touch him, feel his potent male energy.

His dark eyes were closed, his sensual lips slack. A picture of total relaxation except for his cock.

It was wide awake, a giant carved phallic symbol rising upright from his hairless groin. It twitched, as if to say it knew it made her salivate. Her nipples tingled and her breathing grew ragged.

Alexandria sucked the toes on his left foot while Iris undulated beside the couch to the rhythm of the *tabla*.

The heavily beaded bolero Shana wore chafed her nipples, got her even hotter than she'd been before. Needing relief—needing Bear—she started to climb onto the couch.

Selim pulled her back. "You must approach the sheikh from the foot of the bed, my lady."

Shana stared at Alexandria, then at Bear's other foot.

"Okay." Bending, she sucked his big toe into her mouth.

She'd start here, but she intended to make a fast trip to his cock. Or his talented tongue. If she didn't, she'd go berserk.

Shana stroked his foot. His muscular calf. His inner thigh. She followed her hands with her tongue the way she'd done right after they'd boarded his plane, loving the faint smell and taste of sweet almonds on skin as satiny smooth as her own, skin that stretched tautly over powerful male muscles.

The erotic beat of the *tabla*, the high, reedy sounds of some other unseen instrument, and the clicking of coins as Iris danced aroused Shana almost as much as lying at Bear's right side, consuming him inch by inch while Alexandria lay at his other side and continued sucking on his toes.

Allah, but her touch inflamed him. Restraining himself from reaching down and grabbing Shana was as hard as anything Bear had ever done, but he made himself stay still. Maybe if he opened his eyes...

At his eye level, Iris danced the *raks baladi*, or dance of the people. The old ones said watching it would make a dead man's cock rise from within the grave. Bear looked impassively at her undulating hips, not half as turned on by the suggestive movements as by the gentle bites Shana placed along his inner thigh. Or by her warm, damp breath that tickled his freshly denuded ball sac.

His cock strained. His balls tightened.

Alexandria finally let go of his toes and started inching up his left leg. Surprisingly, it didn't take all that much self-control to avoid reacting when her fingers raked his inner thigh.

Her touch should have had him on fire. But it didn't. The gorgeous call girl didn't excite him the way Shana did. He reached down, drew Shana up the bed. "Give me your *yoni*, love," he said, helping her position herself above his hungry mouth, facing his throbbing cock.

"Wait. My clothes—"

"—were made for this." With his hand, he spread apart the crotch of her harem pants and ran his finger along her wet, weeping slit while he aligned his mouth with her throbbing little clitoris and flailed it with his tongue.

"Ohhh."

He loved her familiar taste and smell, the mix of some exotic fragrance and her own unique musk. Her responsive nipples stabbed against his palm when he took the ivory globes, one in each hand. When she strained as if to bend and taste his cock, he held her back.

With his tongue he followed the beat of the *tabla*, alternately stabbing at her clit and lapping up her hot juices as they flowed from her pussy. When he felt the other woman's tongue on his balls, he moved one hand off Shana's breast, insinuated a finger between the folds of her nicely rounded ass.

His finger slippery with her juices, he very gently worked the first knuckle of his index finger past her sphincter muscle. Waited for her to get used to the unfamiliar invasion. Slid in farther.

"I want your cock," she said, squirming against his mouth while he ate her and gently finger-fucked her ass.

Vaguely he noticed the music had stopped. Iris had shed her veils and knelt at the foot of the couch where she licked Alexandria's pussy, while Alexandria sucked Bear's cock and Bear pleasured Shana with his hands and mouth.

He should have been ready to explode.

Instead he wanted the other women gone. He lifted Shana and set her down at his side.

"Don't stop," she whimpered.

He kissed her pouting lips. "I've no intention of stopping, love. The rest of you, get out."

Shana's smile shot through him like an electric shock.

"I want to ride you now," she said, her eyes sparkling with desire and—he hoped—something akin to love.

Bear looked like a man in love. And Shana wouldn't do anything to spoil the illusion. After all, he'd sent the bimbos away and was rubbing fragrant oil into his hands and onto her hard, aching nipples. For the moment he was all hers.

Hers. All nine or ten glorious inches of his hard, hot cock. Slowly she impaled herself on his rigid phallus.

Shana had the rest of him, too, for now.

She circled his small, flat nipples with her fingers, then bent and kissed first one and then the other while she tightened her pussy muscles around his cock. God, but he filled her so completely. Set her on fire. His balls shifted in their velvety sac against her swollen slit.

He cradled her butt in his hands, helping her to set the rhythm. And again, he insinuated an oiled finger up her anus, one knuckle at a time until he got the entire finger inside.

No one had ever touched her like this before. She cried out softly, because it hurt. Yet it felt good, too. Especially when he started moving his finger in and out of her there, maintaining the rhythm she set, riding his huge, delicious cock.

When her climax hit her moments later, she collapsed on Bear's chest, drained, barely registering his triumphant scream when he exploded, his hot semen scalding her wrung-out pussy.

* * * * *

Sunlight streamed through the double doors, making Shana blink. Was it morning already?

She stretched and started to get up when Bear clamped down a muscular arm around her waist. "Stay, love," he mumbled, obviously still half-asleep.

He sent the bimbos away. And he let me sleep with him all night. Like a lover, not a captive houri.

The sheikh of her fantasies had sent her away after taking his pleasure. Why hadn't Bear?

Did he feel more than lust? Would he be sorry when their time together ended? Did he want more?

The idea thrilled her. It also terrified her.

His half-hard cock nudged the back of her upper thighs, as though seeking the warmth of her pussy. Smiling, she let him in, squeezing her thigh muscles gently around him.

He grew rock-hard between her legs, and that got her horny again. When he took her breast in his big hand and stroked it, moisture pooled between her legs.

Hot. He was hot and silky and huge now. Close to her aching pussy but not quite there.

Shana shifted to her belly, tugged his hand to urge him to come along.

His muscular chest pressed hers into the colorful cushions. His warm, moist breath tickled the back of her neck. Then he nipped her with his teeth and sent more waves of sexual longing through her.

His big hands were on her hips now, lifting her to her knees. His cock probed her, its hot, blunt head nudging her anus.

She gasped. No way could he fit his monster cock in there!

"Don't be afraid, love. This is not the hole he seeks." He shifted position and found her pussy. "He craves the tightness, the heat, the wetness here," he whispered as he slid home.

Slow. Maddeningly slow. But so deep that each time he sank his cock inside her all the way he touched her womb. Shana moaned. Yes, she wanted fantastic sex with this man, but she wanted so much more.

The way he fucked her as though he cherished her, taking his time stroking her, nibbling her with his teeth and sampling her with his tongue, gave evidence that he wanted more, too.

Her climax began this time deep within her body, a tiny rumble that bubbled up, grew, and blossomed into a firestorm of sensation when his cock grew impossibly larger and harder before he, too, shouted his triumph.

"Why did you keep me with you last night?" Shana asked a long time later as she lay sated in Bear's arms.

He smiled, though his expression spoke more of regret than of happiness. "Because, love, I've decided your fantasy must become our reality."

Chapter Four

ഗ

"For how long?" Shana asked, her eyes as bright as her words were brittle.

Bear traced around one of her dark-rose nipples with his finger. "Forever, love."

"That's impossible. Our families—"

"Our families will have to accept us if you want this, too."

"It will never work. Your life is here, mine is in Texas."

The regret in her eyes gave Bear reason to press on. "It will work if we want it to. Give us a chance."

"I would never accept you having dozens of wives."

"Four. That's the most the Prophet allows," he countered, grinning.

Shana raked her nails gently down his back. "One is the most I'd allow. I don't care what it says in the Koran."

He laughed. "I can live with that so long as she's you. Any more hot *houris* like you, and I'd soon be dead from sexual excess."

"What about them? Your *houris*?"

"What *houris*?"

She pressed her belly into his, capturing his cock between them in a silken vise. "The ones who were dancing for you and sucking on your balls last night."

"I'll get rid of them." Shana didn't need to know they were only props.

Her eyes widened. "Say you won't put them in pillowcases and toss them into the sea."

Bear hugged her. "No, my fanciful one. You've lived in your fantasy world of the Arabian Nights too long if you believe that. I'm no Ottoman emperor, it's not the sixteenth century, and those women aren't my slaves. Besides, we've come a long way toward becoming civilized. Come on. It's past time I showed you how modern Arabs live."

* * * * *

Things were moving too fast. Part of Shana wanted to put on the brakes, remind Bear that they'd agreed the only place their mutual attraction could take them was to bed — and temporarily at that. But in her heart she yearned for the kind of love match she sensed they'd have — if it weren't for the deep chasm that lay between their customs and traditions.

Her mind was still jumbled a half-hour later when she climbed into a small, twin-engine plane at an airstrip near the villa. Shaking her head, she tried to get it into focus. She'd actually agreed to marry Bear, divide their lives between here and Houston. He promised her the exclusive use of his cock. And she said she'd join him when he sprang the news on his parents. Terrified of what lay ahead, she fastened her seatbelt and hung on to the chair arms while Bear took off.

He flew the plane the way he fucked, flawlessly and with his full attention on the controls. Before she managed to work out the conflicts in her mind, they landed at the airport in Kuwait City and taxied to a hangar emblazoned with Arabic words she assumed named Bear's father's oil company. Sparing a few words for the ground crew that met the plane, Bear whisked her away to a waiting limousine.

He had on a beautifully tailored pale-gray suit today, the *ghutra* apparently his concession to tradition. She, on the other hand, wore the *abaya*, scarf, and veil. It seemed preferable to one of the skimpy harem outfits that had been her other option.

Bear said a few words to the chauffeur before joining her. "First stop, the boutique where my mother buys her clothing. I want to get you out of that *abaya*." With a grin, he dipped his hand inside it and cupped her mound. "But perhaps I should keep you in it so I can touch you like this."

"It's not fair when you don't open yourself the same way to me." His desert robe provided easier access than pants for her to play with his big, smooth cock and balls.

He tweaked her clit. "When I wear a robe, it's usually over western clothes. Yesterday I wanted to give you a special treat. Look around. How different is this from Dallas or Houston?"

"Not very." Date palms and globe-shaped streetlights lined a smoothly paved street. Modern buildings housed stores with window displays of goods one might buy anywhere in the world. Only a few traditionally dressed shoppers and two gorgeous golden obelisks rising in the distance against a bright blue sky set the scene apart from upscale shopping districts back home.

A few minutes later, wearing a pale blue dress by Balenciaga, Shana looked around at an off-white villa that would have been equally at home in River Oaks. The confrontation looming on the horizon made her tremble.

Bear took her left hand, twisted around the massive dark-blue sapphire surrounded by twinkling diamonds that he'd put there moments earlier. The ring weighed heavier on Shana's heart than on her hand.

"It will be all right, love. My mother will support us."

Diana el Rashid was British. She might be sympathetic — at least until Bear mentioned Shana's religion. But his father would probably have a brain hemorrhage from the get-go.

Not unlike the hemorrhages Mother and Daddy were likely to have when they got the news.

"This isn't going to work," she said, panicking when he stepped back to let her go first into a foyer laid with hand-painted tiles that must have cost zillions of Kuwaiti *dinars*. Shana had no doubt that the jewels embedded in a gold statue on the antique table were costly and real. As real as the bowing servant who'd opened the heavily carved wooden entry door.

Owning miles and miles of desert filled with oil wells had to be profitable beyond anything in her experience, and she was raised with wealth. The villa and everything in it spoke silently of unlimited assets and impeccable taste.

"Mother loves me. She will love you, too," Bear said quietly, giving her hand a squeeze.

Shana forced a smile. Some of her terror evaporated when a slender dark-haired woman enveloped Bear in a fierce hug.

"My son. Welcome home. You must introduce me to your friend."

Bear beamed at his mother. "Mother, this is Shana Green. My fiancée."

Shock registered momentarily on the older woman's face, but she recovered quickly and gave Shana a hug. "Welcome," she said. "Come, I must hear all the details. Dahoud, your father will want to meet Miss Green before you go back to that crumbling mass of stones you insisted that Asad open up for you. If you wish to live there, we will have to arrange for its renovation."

"I imagine my work will keep me in Kuwait City much of the time," Bear said, his expression troubled. He smiled at Shana. "We will spend part of each year in Texas so Shana will not miss her family too much."

Would Bear's loving her cost him his place as his father's heir? Shana hoped not. She couldn't even offer him the security of becoming a part of GreenTex if his father turned him out.

* * * * *

"My father has not disowned me," Bear told Shana the next morning when they had boarded the plane to return to Texas—and what he imagined would be a tense confrontation with Shana's parents. "He has, however, suggested that I remain in Texas for a while. Study for a master's degree, perhaps."

"Because of me?"

"Not entirely. The Emir fears an attack from Saddam Hussein. If Iraq attacks, we could be in great danger."

"Would you have to fight?" Shana's eyes widened, and her knuckles were white from clenching her fists.

"No. I would not have to fight. I am an only son, my father's only heir. Should Kuwait have to fight for its existence, though, I would choose to join my countrymen in the military."

"Flying planes?"

"Not unless I got some combat training. Flying the jet fighters the Emir has bought from your country is, I imagine, quite different from flying the Cessna I brought up from *Mina Su'ud*. I would more likely be given some minor command over troops guarding our desert oilfields."

Shana shuddered.

"Come here and let me love you. Let us not think now of events which may never happen." He patted the seat beside him, and when she sat down he took her in a fierce embrace.

She trembled in his arms. So small yet so strong. She'd stood up to his disapproving father when he suggested she had Zionist leanings, fire in her dark eyes, and said she was an American, no more aligned with the rulers of Israel than she was with his own Emir. She'd sworn she loved Bear and would honor the traditions of his heritage and his faith even though they were not her own.

"I was proud of you, love, for your courage in facing my father. May I be as strong when I face your parents." He looked out a window and repressed a pang of regret when he saw the minarets atop the mosque adjacent to the old *souk*. How long would it be before he'd see his home again? "Have you spoken with Jake?"

"I called him last night. He said he'd talk to Mom and let her know about us, so hopefully the shock will have worn off before we get there."

"I like your brother." Besides being competitive and personable, the teenager seemed to have his priorities straight, something many American college boys didn't. "Will he be able to soothe your family's objections?"

"He's an only son, too, and spoiled rotten. If anybody can bring Mom around, it's Jake. Daddy has always expected a lot from Jake, more than he's ever asked for from me or my sisters. He also listens more to whatever Jake has to say."

Bear sighed. He looked forward to informing Jacob Green he intended to spirit his youngest daughter half a world away into a society totally different from what she knew, even less than he'd relished telling his father he would marry a foreigner and a Jew.

After all, he doubted he would like it twenty years from now if some foreigner came along, wanting to steal his little girl away.

But he couldn't be less intrepid than Shana.

Setting aside his worries for the moment, Bear nibbled at her ear. His cock still protested the loss of her company in his bed last night, but he could hardly have risked sneaking into the room next door to his parents' suite where his mother ushered Shana as soon as they agreed to spend the night.

Since he had the feeling opportunities for sex would be as limited in her parents' home if not more so, he decided to take his pleasure now, away from the prying eyes of questionably well-meaning parents. "I want you," he said, dragging her hand to his zipper.

"What did you do about the bimbos?"

"They're gone. Along with Selim. Back to wherever Asad found them."

Shana laughed when he explained the lengths to which he'd gone so she could live her fantasy. Then she let him carry her to the bedroom where she stripped down and fingered the ruby in her navel.

"You're going to have to get me a sapphire like this one for my belly button, I think," she said, looking first at her engagement ring and then at the large ruby. "Yes, I know you are. It can be my wedding present."

"I will give you your weight in them if you wish it, love." His *houri*. Soon to become his only wife.

"I want you to fuck me now. We can talk about jewelry later."

He dropped his pants and boxers, and clasped his swollen cock in his hand. "You want this?"

"Oh, yes." Sinking to her knees, she swirled her tongue around the distended knob, then took him in her mouth and applied gentle suction. God, how she loved cupping his tight ass cheeks, running her finger down the crack and around his puckered anus before cupping his velvety scrotum and gently rolling his balls between her hands.

He burrowed his fingers into her hair to hold her head to his groin. Or to pull her away. Allah, grant him control to savor this a few minutes longer!!

Bear struggled to hold off his climax. The sight of her kneeling before him had him close, and feeling her hands and mouth on him like this nearly did him in.

Closing his eyes, he silently recited periodic tables and let the waves of sensation carry him closer to the edge, until she let go of his cock and took his balls into her mouth one at the time. Her tongue felt like velvet on his ball sac.

When she sucked his cock back down her throat, he nearly exploded. And the unfamiliar sensation of her finger slowly sliding up his ass made his balls draw up in their sac.

He had to stop her now.

"Later, love," he said, freeing his cock and replacing it with his voracious mouth.

With his tongue, he fucked her mouth the way he wanted to fuck her hot, wet pussy.

"Fuck me. Now. Please." She broke the kiss, lay back on the bed. Her dark hair glowed against jewel-toned pillows, and her pale, creamy sex glistened. The muted lights seemed to turn the ivory tones of her satiny body to burnished gold, her nipples and swollen clit to dusky rose.

Shana aroused him more than a thousand *houris*. She was the woman he loved.

He couldn't resist pausing to lap her honey, even though his cock was ready to burst. And when he joined their bodies and shared her shuddering climax, he finally knew the meaning of making love.

Chapter Five

๛

It was more than sex. More than wanting Bear's beautiful cock in her pussy, her hands and mouth all over his magnificent body.

Shana finally knew how it felt to be in love. But what if her mom and dad made her choose between them and Bear?

She'd made her choice the day before yesterday when she held out her hand for him to put this magnificent ring on her finger. But she didn't want to lose her family.

Clutching Bear's hand nearly a day after they'd left Kuwait City, Shana stepped from the plane and glanced at the GreenTex Petroleum logo on a hangar, then back at the big jet with the strange Arabic symbols Bear said meant "El Rashid."

None of the ground crew or customs inspectors seemed surprised to see the unfamiliar plane. One inspector even asked to be remembered to Bear's father.

Maybe the world had shrunk enough that their marrying wouldn't make it shatter. Shana hoped so.

Then she saw her brother.

"Look, there's Jake. That must mean Mother and Daddy are willing to hear us out."

"It will be all right, love. The worst will be that they won't throw you the society wedding of the year."

On the way home, Jake bolstered her spirits further. "Remember what the Old Man always said about people being people, no matter where they come from or what they believe or whether they're rich or poor, every time he caught me joining in to tease some kid at school?"

"I remember you getting grounded for two weeks for calling a classmate some derogatory name. But what does that have to do with us now?"

"Pop mumbled it to himself, sort of, after I mentioned Bear's Kuwaiti and Muslim. Almost like he was reminding himself what he believes. I don't think you'll get much hassle."

Bear wasn't certain of that until Jacob Green called him into his study and repeated the philosophy he said he had developed while acting as a translator for the war crimes tribunal following World War II. "Will you take care of Shana?" was the only pointed question he asked.

"I will protect her with my life," Bear replied without hesitation.

"Then you have my blessing."

Epilogue

Their wedding took place three days before the Butcher of Baghdad attacked Kuwait. Shana clung to Bear the morning Iraq invaded, but she'd known since learning the Emir had fled to the United States that this was coming.

The Gulf War raged for five long months. Kuwaiti oil fields burned for many months after Saddam's forces were defeated. Through it all, Bear served his country while Shana prayed for him from her childhood home.

Though Bear's plane went down, he escaped unscathed and came back to Shana. Together they built their dream home near *Mina Su'ud*, on the site of the ancient villa the Iraqi army destroyed, finishing it in time to welcome their first child, a daughter.

Desert sand and blue sky framed nearby el Rashid oil fields rebuilt with GreenTex technology. To the east lay the *Khalij*, no longer floating with oil slicks by the time Shana presented Bear with their second daughter two years later.

The years passed quickly, and on the eve of their eleventh anniversary, Shana gave Bear a son. Only her worry about her little brother dimmed her joy.

When they came back to Houston a few months later because of her father's illness, Shana vowed to help Jake find happiness again, the way he had paved the way with their parents for her and Bear. Jake needed a good woman—one who'd love him the way she loved Bear, make him a home, and give him the children she knew he would adore.

They lay in bed in their Houston condo, their children asleep with their nanny watching over them. "You know," she said, "I think Kate will be the one for Jake."

Idly, Bear plucked at her swollen nipple. "What makes you so sure?"

"Because Jake gets hard for her the way you still get hard for me," she said, stroking his tightening balls. "Come here. I want to play with your big, beautiful cock."

Forever Enslaved

৯০

Prologue

"You may leave me, my darling, but you will always be mine. My slave, forever enslaved by the love we share."

The words he had said so fiercely to her had the power of Allah's Truth. He knew it in the tears that she shed, the ache and fury in his heart. But still, she had boarded the plane. Now the words echoed off the tarmac, mocking him as the plane sped down the runway, taking away the woman who meant more to him than life.

All he had left of her now was the fine white jet trail that lingered against a brilliant Kuwaiti sky. And she'd taken his heart as well as their two little girls. Dahoud el Rashid tightened his fists, because if he hadn't, he'd have plowed them into the nearest person, place or thing to cross his path. It made no sense. He controlled the lives of thousands who depended on his oil companies for their living, but it seemed he was unable to control his wife—the only one who actually mattered.

She'd insisted he no longer loved her. That he constantly put not only his business but also his ongoing search for relatives missing since the Gulf War ahead of their marriage. She'd told him it nearly killed her every time he made forays across the border, searching for his cousin Jamil and other Kuwaiti officers who'd been missing and presumed captured since the Gulf War had ended ten years earlier.

"I can't live like this anymore, in constant fear that I'm going to get a phone call to tell me you're dead or missing. And I can't stay here for months on end, not able to communicate with anybody but the girls while you're away. Daddy's company has a plane

leaving for the States tomorrow. I'm getting on it and taking the children home. To Houston. You're welcome to come visit them anytime you'd like."

She'd been standing naked on their balcony when she said it, her softly spoken words muffled by the waves lapping against the shore of the Persian Gulf that lay behind them. He'd turned her to him, kissed away each tear, taken her again under the curtain of a star-lit sky. She'd given herself freely as she always had. But in the morning she'd packed and asked him to fly her and his daughters here—so they could leave him.

He realized now he shouldn't have tossed off her threat as just another bit of female hysteria. But he had. He hadn't truly believed she'd go, not until he'd put them on the Green-Tex company jet that even now was winging its way to Texas.

For a long time, Dahoud stood on the tarmac in the blistering August heat, barely aware of it or of the sandstorm brewing in the desert to the south and west. Then he turned on his heel and strode to the el Rashid company hangar.

He knew she still loved him, that he was her center, her heart. He understood he'd been away too much, left her lonely, made her doubt she was still the most important person in his life. Damn it, he should have seen her giving in to quiet despair, realized her concern about his absences and the risks he took were symptoms of loneliness and self-doubt, not the petulant complaints of a spoiled woman used to getting her way.

He'd give her a week. No more. She'd wanted him to capture her years ago, to bring her harem fantasy to life. Well, he intended to capture her now, for real. Holding onto his composure for the benefit of the flight scheduling manager, he arranged to have an el Rashid company jet readied for a transatlantic flight next Tuesday.

No way was he going to let Shana go.

Chapter One
Houston, five days later

ಸಿ

"If you're so lonesome here, why don't you stay at our parents' place?" Shana's younger brother Jake Green grinned, but his tone revealed that Shana's decision to come back to Houston without her husband disturbed him. "You know, I don't think you're being fair to Bear. Oil companies don't exactly run themselves. Besides, the fact that Jamil and Asad are still missing eats at him. You shouldn't blame him for doing everything he can to find them."

"Men. They're all the same. I'd expect nothing more from Jake than that he'd stand up for your selfish brute of a husband." Jake's wife Alice shook her head, tossing her shoulder-length blonde mane as she shot Jake a none-too-pleasant smile. "Jake's off to some filthy oilfield or other almost every week. Someday he'll understand how you feel—when he comes home from one of his jaunts and finds me gone."

"We're not talking about us, Allie." Jake's tone was short. The brief interchange made Shana wonder if his marriage might be on shaky ground.

She hoped not. Her little brother deserved a good life, not grief from the blonde beauty queen-slash-Aggies cheerleader who'd latched onto him his senior year in college. Shana had a moment of discomfort when she realized the shallow woman was taking her side. "I'm staying here because this is my home." *Because I feel Bear's presence in every room and I'm not quite ready to let him go.* "Because the girls are used to us staying here when we're in Houston."

She wished Jake had come alone so she could have poured out her heart to him. She'd never warmed to Alice, any more than Alice had to her. And Shana hadn't left Bear because he had to go and work, the way Alice had suggested she might do. Shana wasn't selfish. She wasn't. Her situation was entirely different. Wasn't it? A shadow of doubt crossed over her, made her not so comfortable with her decision.

As though he'd read her mind, Jake strode over and sat by her on the sunken conversation pit in front of the window. "Bear will come around, sis."

She shook her head. "I don't know. I just needed to get away. I couldn't stand it anymore. He doesn't understand what it's like, what I've tried to tell him." *Once I was inside his heart, his mind. If I was hurting this way, he'd know and understand. Make it better.* At Alice's bored sigh, Shana made herself smile. "I'm not necessarily getting a divorce, Jake. It's okay. I'll be fine here."

Jake slid an arm around Shana, leaned closer, spoke softly into her ear. "I'd have left Allie home, but she insisted on tagging along. Hang in there. I'll be gone a week or so—I have to fly out tomorrow to see if I can solve a problem that's come up in one of our Saudi fields. Frankly I imagine Bear will be here before I get back. I know how he looks at you, and I'd bet he won't countenance being without you for more than a few days."

"Okay." After another half hour of small talk, Shana found herself walking Jake and Alice to the door, saying goodbye and returning to the windows to stare out at Houston's glittering skyline.

She dreaded the long night ahead. It wasn't so bad in the daytime when Yasmin and Selena demanded her attention, but after dark the loneliness ate at her. It hadn't even been a week since she'd left Bear standing on the tarmac, looking as though he'd lost his best friend.

She felt as though she'd lost hers.

They'd been more than lovers from the very first, more than friends. Shana recalled that terrifying night when they'd still been on their honeymoon, when the Iraqi army had invaded Kuwait and he'd told her he had to join the fight. Tears came to her eyes when she remembered a day not long after he'd left her with her parents, when he'd called and told her Jamil's plane had been shot down. There had been sad times along with the joyous ones, but they'd stood together, sharing it all...bound by the love she'd believed would never fade.

No, it wasn't just that her pussy felt empty, neglected. Or that she missed the warmth of her husband's big, muscular body when she woke during the night. It was that she wanted more—so much more—from Bear than he seemed willing or able to give. She wanted them to regain the closeness it seemed had eroded over time, like shifting sands after a storm.

Jake had a point though. El Rashid Petroleum Enterprises could hardly run itself. It was more diversified than her own family's independent oil company, and for the past year or so Bear had taken over a lot of the duties his father had handled before going into semi-retirement. She wasn't so shallow as to resent Bear doing what he had to, to keep the company running smoothly. After all, it provided their livelihood.

The occasional twenty-hour work days he put in wouldn't have been intolerable if only he hadn't also regularly risked his foolish neck, sneaking in and out of southern Iraq—often on camelback with nothing more to protect him than a couple of oil workers and some wicked-looking guns—every time a new rumor surfaced about the possible whereabouts of Kuwaiti prisoners who'd never been freed by the Iraqis after the Gulf War had ended.

No, Shana hadn't signed on to become a widow before she saw the dark side of thirty-five. She could have stood taking second place to her husband's work if it were necessary, but she wasn't about to stand by and sweat whether he'd come back in one piece from the next search in the unforgiving desert. His latest secret, futile, incredibly dangerous mission across the Iraqi border had been the final straw—the incident that had made her call Daddy and say she wanted to come home.

For nearly two weeks she'd wakened every night with the same nightmare. She'd tried to explain every time Bear called how it panicked her, dreaming he lay in the desert, bloodied and broken, bolting upright in bed only to realize it was the same dream. A terrifying prophecy for her—but for him a reason to laugh and assure her he would come home intact.

That hadn't been the first time the premonition had struck her that Bear would someday leave her alone with their daughters in a land of strangers, many of whom viewed her at best with eyebrows-raised suspicion, worst as an age-old enemy to be feared and scorned. A land where she couldn't speak the language or understand it beyond a few simple words, no matter how hard she'd tried.

She'd told no one but Bear why it was that after ten years she'd managed to learn to read and write the language fluently but still couldn't speak or understand it. How the language processing disability she'd had since childhood made it almost impossible for her to "hear" foreign sounds. She'd hired and fired a dozen tutors—and still she could communicate verbally only in her native language.

She'd tried to fit in. And she'd tried hard to talk with Bear, make him understand why she needed reassurance that he'd always be there—that he'd take care never to desert her, whether by design or by accident. Finally she'd come to the conclusion that she'd rather be lonely all the time than terrified and uncertain every time he left the villa to take off on another quest for justice.

Why was it that loneliness clouded her mind now, made her doubt she'd made the right decision?

Like it or not, Shana expected to get far more lonely while Jake was gone. He was the only one of her siblings with whom she felt really close, and she saw a certain irony in the fact that he was about to head out to Saudi Arabia where he'd be more accessible to Bear than to her. Though she loved her sisters, Leah and Deb had been grown by the time she hit her teens and they'd never had all that much in common. Besides, Leah had no time for anything at the moment except her work as a psychological counselor and last-minute preparations for her wedding that was to take place in less than three weeks.

As for their parents, Dad was more of a workaholic than Bear, and Mom had never been particularly sympathetic to Shana's complaints other than to say she needed to "cope". Coping, to Mom, meant immersing herself in charity projects — or flying off to shop and take in the shows in New York, where she was now with Daddy's Mama Anna, shopping for gowns to wear to Leah's wedding.

Shana picked up the phone and punched the memory code for Bear's sister Alina, who was here in the States, just starting her ophthalmology residency. For the fifth straight time, she got Alina's voice mail. The hospital people must have been keeping her running twenty-four, seven for her not to have even returned Shana's calls.

Alone. Damn it, it seemed she was destined to be just as lonely here as she'd been at the villa in *Mina Su'ud* while her husband had tended to his dangerous business — and here everybody spoke English. Restless, she paced around the condo, checking on the girls even though she'd looked in on them less than fifteen minutes ago. She paused for a minute and looked out on the Houston skyline before sinking onto the large antique fainting couch that commanded the living room. When she hugged one of the jewel-toned cushions to her breasts, the faint scent of Bear's musky cologne filled her nostrils.

Everywhere she looked she saw reminders of him. Even this couch...

He used to lie down on it and hold out his arms to her, lifting her over his hard, fit body. She'd straddled him, nibbling his muscular neck, teasing him with her pussy until he got impatient, growled and slammed her down on his cock, hard. Their lovemaking on nights like that had been explosive, but afterward he'd held her, petted her, made her feel cherished...complete.

The couch just wasn't the same without her big, sexy sheikh lounging on it, his dark eyes full of the intense desire that hadn't waned since they'd played out her harem fantasy years ago. Until recently. For the past few months, between Bear's work and his obsessive following of yet more dead-end leads about his cousin and secretary's whereabouts, he'd been coming home so infrequently—and so exhausted—their sex life had begun to suffer almost as much as their relationship.

Not that he couldn't still turn her on with just a look...a touch. But lately he'd often rolled away after they made love, leaving her missing the heat of his body, the tender touch of his hands as they tangled in her hair, as he drew her to him for a long, gentle kiss. Shana lay back on the couch, tossing aside the pillow she'd been holding, and imagined...

The exotic, erotic dissonance of reed instruments, the beat of a tabla. *A tent set in a lush oasis beneath date palms swaying in a welcome desert breeze. She floated there, not on a company jet but a magical carpet, transported beyond Houston, beyond the home she'd shared with Bear and their daughters at* Mina Su'ud *on the* Khalij. *Beyond the pain and the worry, and the realities of bridging schisms in culture and religion to reach the fantasy world she'd once imagined. The fantasy world she and Bear had managed for most of the past ten years to make their own reality.*

Shana's pussy grew wet, needy. She slid her hand along the curves of her body, ran her fingers through her hair the way Bear always did. Closing her eyes, she imagined he was here, his hand on her throat, holding her as he suckled her breasts, first one and then the other. Her nipples hardened almost painfully, but when she touched them she found no relief. She rubbed her clit, pretending it was her husband caressing her, whispering words of love and passion, his excellent English mixed with the Arabic she'd never managed to master well enough so they could share a meaningful conversation.

"You're my love slave. You'll always be mine. Forever enslaved by the love we share."

His parting words rang in her ears. An arrogant claim, typical coming from the powerful sheikh he was. Compelling. She'd always loved his macho self-assurance—that's what had attracted her to him in the first place, beyond the fact she'd wanted him to fulfill the sexual fantasy that had consumed her for so long. Still, she'd seen and loved another side of Dahoud el Rashid. She'd witnessed the man who agonized over the loss of his friends and countrymen, who had wept with pure joy at first sight of his daughters. He didn't show that side to many people, but with her, he'd always let his emotions run free.

Her Bear. Lover, husband, doting father who'd never uttered a word of disappointment that she hadn't given him the son all powerful men seemed to want, to carry on their names, their heritage. She'd been afraid of his reaction, worried that he wouldn't love their daughters the way she did — but he'd surprised her, confirmed their love again as he always had.

Until recently. He'd turned his back on her loneliness and fears about losing him, much as a parent might have brushed aside the absurd fears of a child. At the same time he'd tenderly cured Selena of her fear of the dark, spending hours explaining to their little girl that the darkness was her friend…that he would allow no harm to come to her or Yasmin — or Shana herself. Why could he not have pulled her into her arms when she'd been afraid, soothed her with fairy tales so convincingly she would have believed them, as Selena had?

When he'd held her, she would have believed anything he said. Problem was, the holding lent itself to lovemaking, not talking. Hot, imaginative lovemaking that drove away thoughts of everything else. Shana shuddered at the jolt of sexual need that slammed into her when she remembered having him on her, in her. Fucking her with wild abandon or incredible tenderness, worshiping her body with his strong hands, his sensual mouth…filling her with his huge, beautiful cock.

God, how she wanted him now, to ease the ache her hands couldn't begin to relieve.

How in the name of her God and his Allah had she ever thought she could walk away? When her body ached like this, she couldn't bring to mind all the reasons she'd felt she had to get on that Green-Tex plane and fly away home. Perhaps Jake had been right in saying there was something more that had made her get on that plane, a pain she couldn't face enough to analyze right now, when her ache for Bear seemed to override everything else.

* * * * *

She'd asked him to spend more time in Houston, but fuck it, this was his home. Shana's too. Not their condo in Houston, although Dahoud had always enjoyed spending time there with her and the girls. He paced the marble floor of the salon, stopping in front of the huge expanse of glass that formed one wall of the villa to peer out over the calm waters of the *Khalij*, lit tonight by a bright full moon. In the distance a tanker steamed along, low in the water, bound for Allah only knew where with its load of crude oil.

El Rashid crude? It didn't matter. Not now. All Dahoud could think about was his wife and how he was going to get her back.

If she were here, they'd have been strolling along the water's edge, touching and kissing. She'd have been as bold as he, stopping and meeting his gaze, stroking his cheek, whispering about how much she wanted him. When he pulled her to him, she'd cup his cock through his *dishdasha*, inviting him to lift her caftan and find her hot, wet cunt. His *houri*, she'd called herself on balmy nights like those, when their passions had run hot and hard. When they'd fucked under the sky and again in their bed upstairs, until both of them were too spent to fuck any more. Afterward they'd slept in each other's arms.

Allah, but he missed waking to the soft sound of her breathing, the arousing feeling of her curled up against his belly, cradling his cock between her firm, slender thighs. Whether they made love before he left for work or not, knowing she was there for him had given him a feeling of contentment. Since she'd left, he'd gotten hardly a wink of sleep.

Dahoud thought again about that last night before she left, about how they'd made love in the sunken marble bath. His balls tightened when he recalled her soft, full lips on them, her hot wet cunt stretching to take his throbbing cock.

The taste of her tears when she'd told him afterward that she was leaving still lay bitter on his tongue.

If he hadn't been so exhausted he'd have talked her out of leaving. If he'd believed she'd really do it, he'd have done whatever it took to dissuade her. He'd have persuaded her to stay no matter how tired he'd been, no matter how his temples had been throbbing with eyestrain from having spent the past five days on camelback in the desert northwest of the Iraqi border.

Maybe Shana was right. Maybe at this point no one man could do what many Kuwaitis desperate to find missing family members had failed to accomplish in nine long years. This last tip had led to yet another dead-end...a band of wandering nomads whose sighting of downed Kuwaiti pilots had taken place some nine and a half years ago, even though the news had only made its way to Kuwait City late last month.

No matter. He couldn't promise his wife he wouldn't go search for Jamil and Asad again if more rumors surfaced as to their whereabouts. What he could do — and he had already set plans in motion — was delegate some of the routine jobs he performed at work. His father never had. But then his mother had always managed to keep herself occupied with activities that didn't involve his father. So had Shana's mother, from what he'd seen when they'd visited in Houston.

Shana could have immersed herself in community activities, too, but not as easily. In the small community of *Mina Su'ud* she was an oddity — a Jewish American woman who'd learned to read and write Arabic as well as he could, but whose spoken Arabic left much to be desired despite the string of tutors who'd attempted to teach her. Maybe they should move to Kuwait City, keep this villa for vacations...

No. Shana loved the sea, the desert. Unlike his mother, she was disinclined to devote her days to socializing or charity work. Though she'd often accompanied him to Kuwait City and even to Riyadh—he didn't blame her for hating the enforced *hijab* there or the restrictions the Saudis placed on their women—she loved living here, in the home they'd built together on the rubble of the ancient palace where they'd fulfilled her harem fantasy so long ago.

He'd never forget how her eyes had lit up at first sight of the old villa, or the way she'd broken down and cried when they'd gone there after the Iraqis had destroyed it. She'd recovered quickly, though, and insisted they rebuild, saying she had to live in the place where they'd fallen in love. He saw her touch everywhere, in the soaring windows that overlooked the *Khalij*, the courtyard where she'd faithfully reproduced the old garden with its stone pathways and fragrant, colorful flowers. She'd left her fingerprint on every inch of the place. Just as she'd left an indelible mark on his heart.

Fuck the Iraqis for having destroyed the original villa. Fuck them for having made away with six hundred Kuwaiti prisoners and kept them—or killed them—once the Gulf War had ended. Hurting as he had every day since Jamil and Asad had been taken, Dahoud slammed a fist down onto a marble table, welcoming the physical pain that couldn't compare with the hurt in his heart.

Now he had yet another reason for despising his neighbors to the north, because their barbaric actions might have indirectly cost him Shana. Cursing at the pain that radiated from his knuckles all the way to his shoulder and neck, he made his way to their room, where he felt her presence most keenly.

Damn it all, Shana should have understood. She'd stood by him through the years, helped him rebuild what the Gulf War had destroyed. It had only been these last few months that she'd started begging him to do what he could not—give up the quest to find Jamil and the others of his squadron who hadn't returned. What the fuck did she need from him?

He knew Shana to be a compassionate, loving woman who would fiercely protect everyone in her family. Surely she could not believe he should abandon the search for his cousin. But perhaps—he paused, struggling to understand—perhaps it was more than the irrational fear, the nightmares she'd shared with him as they lay in bed the night before she'd left.

The occasional pain he'd seen in her eyes, more often lately when he'd come in and had little to say to her, or when he was involved in his work and didn't have time to spend with her as they had before, sharing meals, long walks, trips to the desert or the city. Could his *houri* have truly believed she had lost his love, been relegated to second place in his heart?

Dahoud sat on the bed they'd shared, considering the possibilities. Shana understood pain, as all women must, but it could be she was unable to articulate what lay behind it. He, idiot that he was, had only heard her criticism without considering its underlying cause.

He couldn't give up the search for his countrymen. His honor wouldn't permit him to. He could, however, let Shana know through her body as well as her soul that he did love her, did consider her irrevocably his own. Forever.

Chapter Two

Dahoud stood, his mind clearer now that he believed he understood more of what had made Shana leave. He started recalling other nights in this room, good nights when they'd made love until dawn then slept in each other's arms. But now was not the time for looking back. He had plans to make—a wife to bring home. And a fierce ache in his balls he had the feeling only his wife could ease. Tossing his *dishdasha* onto an ornately carved chest beside the sleeping couch, Dahoud stretched out across the bed that felt too big and much too lonely without Shana.

He curled his fingers around his cock and imagined it was his wife's tight cunt that gripped him. Although his flesh swelled and hardened, the sensation was more one of desperate need than impending pleasure.

You could have had three more wives. Surely not all of them would have deserted you because you gave them too little attention.

He could have, but he'd promised Shana she would be the only one. Besides, Dahoud had never felt cheated because he'd relinquished the right of every Muslim man who could afford it to take as many as four wives. He had more than enough on his hands keeping one of them happy, as was evidenced by Shana having walked out.

Allah, but he needed release. Forcing thoughts of his absent wife from his head, he stroked his cock, imagined…an *houri* sucking it while two others stroked his feet and a third straddled his face. All of them had Shana's angel face, her slender curves. Pressure built in his balls. He jerked himself harder. Arghh. Almost. Oh, fuck, there it was, the flood of hot seed into his imaginary *houri*'s mouth.

Spurt after spurt spewed onto his belly, jerking him back into reality. The reality that if he didn't get up, Shana's favorite bed cover was going to be stained with come. Grabbing the *dishdasha* he'd discarded earlier, he clutched it to his midsection before stumbling into the shower.

Six days. Never again would he allow her out of his sight this long! Though Dahoud could provide his own release, only Shana could give him a feeling of true satisfaction—of completion.

* * * * *

Eight days without her husband and she was ready to climb walls. Shana shook her head at Maria, the designer salon manager at Saks. She couldn't get interested in looking at the gowns in Dior's millennium collection with her sister Deb, any more than she'd been able to entertain herself earlier while replenishing Yasmin and Selena's nearly outgrown wardrobes.

"That yellow gown would be perfect for you, Shana," Deb commented before turning to the hovering manager. "I'll try the blue sari and that black suit, please, Maria."

Shana sighed. "I guess I'm not much company today. I'm going home. Are you sure it's no trouble for you to keep the girls overnight?"

"Of course it's no trouble. Lenore and Tracy love having their cousins over. Come on, Shana. You're not a child. Either forget Bear and get on with your life, or go back to him and resign yourself to sharing him with his job and whatever else it is he does that cuts into his time with you. Be glad he hasn't taken on another wife or two—God knows he could afford to support several more like you." Deb stared at the small stack of parcels stacked beside Shana's chair and shook her head.

Maybe Deb was right. But there was no way in hell Shana could forget her husband. There was also no way for her to give in and go home without Bear assuring her the situation would change for the better. After all, she was the one who'd said she couldn't take the uncertainty and loneliness, who'd made up her mind that she couldn't stay and watch their love erode little by little, like a beach ravaged by storms. It was she who'd packed herself and her daughters and flown away, she who had stood before the man she loved more than life and told him they were through. Unless...

Unless he gave her no choice.

Tossed over his shoulder in a silk sack, she had no alternative but to submit when he hefted her over his broad shoulders and spirited her away to an ancient harem on the Khalij. *Mesmerized by the force of his will, she took what had been her most secret fantasy and let him make it a reality.* Nothing—not the cultural and religious differences that would have ground most lovers to a painful parting, nor the short but brutal war that had intruded on their honeymoon—had stood in the way of her following her Arab sheikh.

Except that now she'd gone and left him, and she'd left her heart behind. As Shana got into her car and headed back to the condo, she decided she could grieve there as well as anywhere...and possibly search her heart to see if she could conceive of a way she could accept and balance the pain of being second in his life, as opposed to living with the agony of not having him at all. *Come after me, Bear. Give me no choice. Make me believe in our love again.*

Strange, how what had seemed an impossible life two weeks earlier looked so much better now that she'd tossed it away.

Too bad she still had too much pride to crawl.

* * * * *

Too bad she'd made him go to these extremes.

Dahoud paced across the jewel-toned Persian rug Shana had chosen for the salon of the new El Rashid company jet, air phone in hand. Methodically, as he did with other crucial matters, he arranged the encounter he had in mind to show his wife she still was his love slave—as he was hers. Another hour and he'd be landing in Houston, most likely on the same runway where the predecessor to his company's 767 had landed ten years ago when he'd come home with her to meet her parents and announce they intended to bridge the huge gap between their cultures and become man and wife.

"Yes, Deb. I do intend to win your sister back, but to do that I need to have some time alone with her. I will appreciate your having Shana send my daughters' nanny over to help take care of Yasmin and Selena. Tell the girls we will call them every day." Panic began to set in after Dahoud hung up the phone. What if Shana truly wanted to be free? What if she no longer craved a dominant male who would sweep aside her every objection and take her to heights she'd never reached before?

No. That could not be. He wouldn't allow it. Grasping a handful of silk scarves she'd stashed in a drawer of the bedside table on their first trip in this plane, he imagined using them to tie her to the couch…tasting every inch of her lush body while she writhed in ecstasy beneath his hands and mouth…filling her cunt with his cock and bringing them both to pleasure.

His cock hardened painfully against the fly of his western jeans. He chafed against the pressure, but neither Arab garb nor business suit would work for the scenario he had planned to woo his wife. She'd come home to the land of cowboys—and he had painstakingly planned to show her who was master—Texas style.

*****

That night in their Houston condo, Shana lay naked on the big bed where she'd spent so many rapturous nights with Bear. The exotic, erotic Middle Eastern music she'd loaded onto the stereo echoed in her ears. Sweet-smelling incense swirled about her, the thin cloud of smoke the stick emitted reminding her of a genie rising from Aladdin's magic lamp. Eyes closed, she stroked her clit and twisted her nipples in a desperate search for release.

It wasn't working. Her hands weren't calloused like his. All her own touch did was stoke her need for her husband who was God only knew how many thousand miles away.

Thousands of miles, though they could be bridged in mere hours by a big jet airplane. She could…no, she couldn't hop on the next flight to Kuwait City and go back home. More important, she couldn't give in and sentence herself to decades of taking a distant third place to Bear's job and his compulsive quest to find Jamil and the others.

Still she felt his presence here, in their Houston condo where he hadn't set foot for nearly a year. *Right.* Shana had almost forgotten he'd bailed for the past two years on his promise before they'd married that they'd spend at least three months of every year in Houston, near her friends and family. It had nearly slipped her mind, too, that he'd left her to spend a great deal of that time at the *Mina Su'ud* villa without him, with nothing to do but play with the girls and practice her atrocious Arabic with the servants.

Had she just heard the soft thud of a door closing? Footsteps? She must have been losing her mind. She was alone. Completely alone. Even the girls' nanny was gone, summoned earlier in the evening by Deb to help with Yasmin and Selena while they visited with her daughters.

Those sounds kept getting closer…louder, though muted. Yeah, they would be, wouldn't they? She'd insisted the carpets here be thick, soft, so deep a footprint lingered for hours. *Did I forget to set the burglar alarm? No, I activated the damn alarm system when I came back this afternoon. No one's here. It's got to be my imagination.*

There was no use trying to put out the fire in her pussy. None at all. Maybe a glass of milk would help her sleep. Shana rolled off the bed, padded across the room and groped for a robe.

"Do not cover yourself, *houri*. I wish to see you as Allah made you."

Not daring to breathe for fear of spoiling the fantasy, Shana started to turn toward the sound of the familiar, much-loved voice, but before she could see him, something soft slid over her head. "Bear?"

She reached out to touch his cheek, expecting her fingers to brush against the fine cotton of his *ghutra*. Instead she encountered the rolled brim of a Stetson. "Yes, *houri*. It's me. We are about to take a journey. On that journey we will explore the many paths to sexual pleasure you say I have denied you these past few months. I have found a very special dude ranch not far from here. There you will submit to me and love every minute of your enslavement. Never fear, for the next few days you will have my undivided attention, and by the time I return you here, you will want to end this foolish separation."

He drew her close, cupping her breasts, stroking the needy flesh between her legs—and slipping something silky and all-encompassing around her naked body. God but she wanted him to take her, fuck her here and now. Then she remembered she'd left him for good reason and tried to pull away. And their separation might seem foolish to him, but not to her. "No. You can't just come in here and expect me to do whatever you say." She wished her protest hadn't come out sounding so lame.

"I can, and I am."

"The children—"

"Yasmin and Selena will be fine with your sister. When I told Deb of my plan, she most kindly agreed to take them for several days."

"But, Bear—"

"Do not make excuses. Your body tells me you want this—" he rubbed his rock-hard cock against her belly and ran his calloused hands along the curve of her upper arms, "—even if your heart is not so sure. Are you coming peacefully, or must I carry you?"

"Carry me." Every cell in her body ached for him to take her, but Shana dared not give in too easily. If she did, this would be only a short, satisfying interlude before Bear took her home and started all over again with the pattern of work, work, work, interspersed with the frequent sojourns into the desert that kept her petrified with fear that the desert might take him from her. "I never said I didn't like having sex with you, but this doesn't mean I intend to take you back."

"We shall see, my darling wife." Bear's deep, rumbling laugh made her want to pummel him. Still her rebellious pussy creamed and her pulse raced when he lifted her over his shoulder. As powerful now as when he'd been a star linebacker back in college, he hauled her out of the condo as though she weighed no more than a feather.

The elevator lurched into motion. Shana's heart pounded with anticipation even as she let go some of her frustration by flailing at her captor's backside with her fists. As she did, she couldn't help liking the hard, fit feel of him, or remembering how the muscles of his ass cheeks flexed under her fingers when they were making love.

"Go ahead, get the anger out of your system. The only way you can hurt me is by walking out of my life."

She'd walked out—hadn't she? Or had her flight been nothing more than the satisfaction of a temporary fit of insanity? Shana didn't know, but she kept on flailing her arms about as though she could dislodge herself from her husband's iron grip. "Put me down," she ordered, but when he set her on her feet she missed his nearness. His touch.

"Now, *houri*, you may as well sit back and relax, because I am taking you for a long ride. I believe you'll find the journey worth it." With that, Bear urged her onto the front seat of a car and buckled her in.

Chapter Three
Circle B Ranch and Dungeon, between Houston and San Antonio

ଅ

Apparently the proprietors here saw nothing unusual about a man hauling in a woman over his shoulder and checking in without luggage for a three-day stay. Bear set Shana down long enough to sign the registration form, then lifted her again and followed the bellman—a muscular young man in cowboy attire—to the suite he had reserved.

"Perfect," he said when the young man stepped back so he could examine the accommodations. Eyeing the St. Andrew's cross against one wall of the sitting room, he strode to it and deposited his wife before it. "I may require your services later, but for now this will be all." Bear reached in his pocket and handed over a folded twenty-dollar bill.

He turned to Shana once they were alone. "Would you like to see your surroundings, my love?"

"Damn you, get this thing off my face! You tied the knot so tight, I can't get it loose."

Good, he'd made her angry...again. He wanted her mad. Hot. Thinking about how she'd told him she was leaving, so sadly, as though she had given up on caring for him, tore at his soul. This was his chance—his only chance—to change direction for them. He couldn't fail.

For a minute he fumbled with the tie on the hood she wore then gave up and ripped it loose. "You are at my mercy," he said, keeping his voice low, soothing. He lifted the hood but gave her no opportunity to flee, sliding off her robe before grasping both her hands. "I intend to fuck you so well you'll never again be able to so much as think of leaving me."

At the sudden despair he saw warring with her desire, he added, "I also intend to make you believe I worship you. That I cannot live without you." Goaded to raw honesty by his desperation to reach her, he took her hand. "My love slave, my heart is chained to you. Don't you know that?" She shuddered, closed her eyes, and he moved in, caressing her, murmuring endearments first in his language, then in hers. "Look around you. See what pleasures await us."

Shana sputtered when she saw her surroundings. The spanking bench beside the bed and a fucking swing that took up space in an alcove by the window obviously caught her attention, fed her fury. "You—you wouldn't dare!" Bear noticed her staring now at the array of whips and floggers mounted on the wall behind the wet bar.

"Only if you defy me, my love." He couldn't imagine striking her pale flesh, but the fantasy of the threat bloomed before his eyes when he noticed she was shivering, not with fear but with the edge of arousal fear sometimes wrought. Arousal that heated his own blood in answer to her response.

Bear ran his hands up her slender arms, resting them on her shoulders. "I want to bring you pleasure, never to hurt you. We are going to explore some avenues new to both of us—but I promise you nothing but the most exquisite, erotic of pleasures. You're angry with me, so I don't expect you to fall into my arms of your own volition. I expect to work to earn your submission. Back up against the cross."

Her slow intake of breath reverberated through his fingers. Seconds ticked away as she stared at him and he at her. "Make the first move. Show me at least that much trust." If she didn't, he would back off—but then she took one step backward, then another.

When she looked up at him, her eyes glittered. Fear? He didn't think so, for Shana had no reason to be afraid of him. More likely, the thought of making herself helpless to serve his pleasure excited her in spite of her protests. After all, she'd come to him more than ten years ago wanting no more than for him to fulfill the fantasy she'd woven in her head about how life would be in a harem, with her enslaved by her Arab master.

He'd never forget the first time, the heavenly feel of her warm mouth on his cock as she knelt before him in the cabin of an El Rashid company jet at thirty thousand feet. The sparkle in her eyes when she'd begged him to take her would remain engraved in his memory forever. He'd never forget this, either, her slow, seemingly reluctant obedience, as though she wanted to refuse him but could not.

Slowly she raised her arms and rested them against the upper arms of the highly polished wooden cross. When he had them secured, he couldn't resist taking her mouth. Allah, but she tasted sweet, like mint and herbs. A remembered scent from long ago, one implanted in his mind for all time, one he'd always associate with the woman he loved. "I have missed you, *houri*." He knelt, nudging her legs apart and securing her ankles and thighs to the lower arms of the device, pausing to stroke the incredibly soft skin there, determined despite her resistance to elevate her to the heights of the desperate desire that drove him. He nuzzled her satiny mound, finding her clit and giving it a quick nibble.

She tensed, and he saw her clench one fist from the corner of his eye. He flicked her clit with his tongue. "Damn it, I don't want to want you," she ground out. Fighting her own desire? Well, she wouldn't fight it for long. Bear gave her pussy one last love bite before rising.

"Do not fear, my love, I will take care of you." Deliberately he pried off his boots, never losing eye contact.

Shana watched her husband's big, sure hands move to his hand-tooled belt. Resisting him would have been so much easier if she could hate him, but she could not. She couldn't even work up a righteous fury at him for having brought her here and made her helpless to his will. Her pussy clenched with anticipation for what he'd do next. "Aren't you going to undress, cowboy?" she asked, not sounding nearly as mocking as she'd intended.

She wanted him naked, as vulnerable—or almost—as she. Her fingers itched to stroke every inch of his gorgeous, clean-shaven body, to feel the hard muscles rippling beneath baby-soft, supple skin. But he seemed to be in no hurry, sliding his thumbs under the wide leather on either side of the buckle, making no move to do more. When he smiled, she realized he was teasing her. "Get on with it," she snapped.

"You want this?" Freeing one hand, he laid it on the impressive bulge beneath his snug denim jeans.

He knew damn well she did. No way could he not have known. Her clit was hard as rock. Moisture gushed from her cunt. Her nipples tingled. The smell of her arousal hung in the air. "No!"

"Yes, you do. I can tell. Whatever problems sent you running away from our marriage, they had nothing to do with this."

No, it had nearly killed her to leave him, knowing she'd be missing the scorching, imaginative sex that hadn't ever become routine or boring. Too infrequent, yes. But what she'd missed was the cuddling afterward, the sense of emotional oneness that encircled them in a warm, cocooning afterglow. But never, ever boring. She had the feeling walking away would be even harder next time. If she hadn't been bound—for which she admitted she'd given him tacit consent—she'd have run away. Escaped from the inexplicable emotions that kept her tied to this man as surely as he'd bound her to serve his pleasure.

My pleasure, too.

Shana cursed the inner voice that urged her to surrender, take on all the heartache that had invaded their marriage in return for the incredible sensations she knew he'd deliver with his mouth...his hands...his muscular body and huge, beautiful cock. "I want..."

"What is it you want, *houri*?"

"God, I don't know." But she did. She wanted him to take away the pain, envelop her in passion, drive out all her doubts and fears.

With a quick motion, graceful for one so large, Bear loosened his belt, tugged his shirttails out and began to work on unfastening the buttons of his jeans. "You want this. You may not want to want it, but your pussy aches for my cock as surely as it aches for you."

Her mouth watered when his cock sprang free, so big and hard and inviting to her mouth. "Oh, yes," she hissed before she could manage to hold back the words.

"Yes." Quickly now, as if he knew exactly how much she needed him, he stripped off the rest of his clothes and stood before her naked. Fully aroused. Deliciously aroused. "I'm going to fuck you until you scream with satisfaction, but first..." he tilted the cross, bringing her torso level with his shoulders, "first I'm going to touch you. Taste you. Reacquaint myself with every millimeter of your lush, tempting body. By Allah, I have not slept for nine long days but that I've dreamed of you. Of this."

Dipping his head, he took first one nipple and then the other into his mouth and suckled. He used both hands to skim over her throat, her breasts, her belly. Why wouldn't he touch her pussy? Ease the empty ache as only he could?

Shana strained against her bonds, but they held fast. Maybe if she begged...

...but all she could manage to verbalize was a pathetic whimper.

"Relax, love. We've all night. All day tomorrow." He dipped his head again and blew gently on her aching nipple. "We have the rest of our lives."

"No! It was hard enough to leave. I can't go through that again."

"Then do not. Let me show you how good it can be between us. Better even than before you decided I was neglecting you." His treacherous tongue went out, traced a damp, arousing path from her left breast to her navel where he circled the large sapphire belly button ring he'd put there on their wedding night. "Do you remember I offered you your weight in precious jewels?"

"Yes. I'd have settled for having you and not having to worry every time you left whether I'd ever see you again."

"Nothing could keep me from coming home to you, *houri*. But honor demands I follow every lead. If it had not been for me—"

"Don't bring your insane sense of guilt in here. Now's not the time for talking. Stop torturing me and make me come." Shana thought she'd die if he left her like this, bound, aroused and unfulfilled.

"Your wish is my command, my greedy love." Bear's hot breath tickled her mound then made her clit tingle with anticipation when his lips closed around the rigid nub. "Come to your heart's content. I intend to drink my fill of your sweet honey."

She strained against her bonds, needing to tangle her fingers in his glossy black hair, to bind his hot lips to her needy flesh as he'd bound her for his pleasure. He held her helpless against a sensual onslaught she'd never been able to resist. No choice but to submit…to let sensations override her anger, her sense of hurt. No alternative but to let him take her…

"Oh, God! Don't stop." She could no more have held back the words than she could have stopped breathing. When he slid two long fingers up her pussy and moved them slowly in and out, an ache began low in her belly, intensifying as it spread. Her clit felt as though it would explode against his seeking tongue. She was coming, but she wanted more. "Fuck me, damn you."

He straightened, adjusting the angle of the cross so her swollen pussy was level with his throbbing cock. "Is this what you want?"

"Yesss…" Every nerve in her body thrummed with satisfaction yet demanded more.

He rubbed his cock along her wet slit. Slowly. Delicious torture, but she couldn't stand much more. "Fuck me now!"

"Say it in Arabic."

"*Nek ni*. Please. I'm dying inside."

He laughed. "Ten years and you still can't get out more than two words without switching back to English when you're hot for me?"

"Shut up and give me your big cock."

"I shouldn't, but I will."

His heat seared her as the broad head of his cock slowly penetrated her needy pussy. It set off the earlier climax that still held her in its grip, made her strain to take his full length. "I want it all, damn it."

"You're a demanding wench, aren't you?"

"Yes." He sank in another inch, stretching her, making her contract her inner muscles to squeeze the invading flesh. "Oh God!" she cried when he found her G-spot and rubbed back and forth on it with the thick head of his cock. She was coming, still and again, sensations thrumming through her body like a series of shock waves.

He took her mouth, muffling her cries of completion as he slammed full-length into her. Filling her completely. Feeding the climax that left her so drained she barely registered his own shout of triumph, the hot spurts of his seed that bathed her pussy when he came seconds later.

* * * * *

The next morning Dahoud woke refreshed for the first time since Shana had told him she was leaving. Waking with her warm and naked in his arms, sexually sated and relaxed in sleep, was a pleasure he never intended to deny himself again. Fate had brought them together against the odds, and he'd allow nothing to keep him from winning her back, not just for the moment, but for all time.

When he'd freed her from the St. Andrew's cross she'd flowed into his arms without protest, as if she'd known that was where she belonged. Later they'd talk…and he'd listen — really listen this time — to the concerns that had caused her to take their daughters and leave him.

He glanced at the fucking swing, recalled her fantasy about a ménage, his vow after she'd left to make her every dream come true. The idea of suspending her there and watching young studs giving her pleasure while he looked on stirred the streak of possessiveness that shouted she was his alone. It also aroused the hell out of him, imagining her writhing under the hands and mouths of strangers while he orchestrated their every move. He'd have to trust she wanted him more…that the only thing the studs would be giving her was extra mouths and hands. And cocks.

Fuck. No way would he permit any other man to put his cock in his wife's pussy. Anywhere else, either. Dahoud rolled over, ignoring his painful hard-on. If he was going to go through with the ménage he'd arranged for tonight, he needed to get Shana up and out. They had to talk, and he had to convince himself he was the only man she really wanted. Otherwise he couldn't fulfill this fantasy they'd talked about but never played out in real time.

He dressed quickly then laid out some specially designed jeans and a western shirt for Shana. "It's morning, *houri*. Let's get you up, get some breakfast and take a ride."

"Too early," she mumbled, burrowing deeper beneath the covers.

"Come on, sleepyhead. It's riding a horse or riding me." *Or both.* When she didn't sit up immediately he sat beside her and gave her a gentle shake. "You said last night we needed to talk—and we can talk better when I'm not on a bed being distracted by the sight of your gorgeous naked body."

"I don't have any clothes…"

"No excuses. I ordered some for both of us when I made the reservation."

She glanced at the garments he'd laid out by her side. "You forgot about underwear."

"No, my love. I didn't forget. I want your sweet little cunt accessible, and your beautiful breasts free to jiggle and drive me insane."

"All right. Excuse me." With that she rose and headed for the bathroom, hugging the clothes over the front of her torso as though she wanted to deny him the pleasure of looking at her.

For the first time since he'd walked in on her at their condo last night, Dahoud doubted he'd managed to seduce Shana into dropping the crazy idea of leaving him. Her uncharacteristic modesty, coupled with the curt dismissal and a stubborn set to her sensual lips, told him it would take more than hot sex to lure her back.

What the fuck had happened to the days when men were masters and women their willing slaves?

Chapter Four

෨

"I thought you said we were having breakfast first," Shana said when Bear practically dragged her out of the main guesthouse toward the stable.

"We are. It's in this basket I ordered for us to take along. According to the proprietor, there's a private, pleasant spot to dine along a stream. It's about a ten-minute ride on horseback, or so he said. He also mentioned the cell phone reception there is good, so we can call Yasmin and Selena."

Try as she might, Shana couldn't accuse her husband of neglecting their daughters. Even at his most distracted, most exhausted homecomings he'd always made time to play with them, tuck them in their beds. It had been she who had gotten the remnants of his energy, an offhand kiss before his eyes had glazed over and he'd fallen asleep. "All right. I know they've been missing you."

"They'll be wanting to talk with you, too."

"I doubt that. They see me every day. Yasmin couldn't say yes fast enough when Deb offered to have them sleep over and play with their cousins."

"It sounds as though you're jealous," Bear commented as he took the reins of a spirited-looking palomino from a stableboy and led the horse outside. "Here, I will give you a leg up."

She avoided his gaze. "No, not really. It's just…difficult sometimes, to come second. To feel like you're second." She shrugged, shook her head. "It's nothing. A silly feeling. We're riding double?" she asked, settling into an unusually large western saddle, uncomfortable with the look he shot her way.

After a long moment, Bear mounted, his motion efficient and natural, as though he rode horseback every day—even though she knew he hadn't found time lately to exercise his favorite Arabian mare as much as he'd have liked to. "Yes. We're riding double. Do you remember the time I took you on a camel ride in the desert?"

"Oh, yes. I remember." Shana would never forget that day—the rocking motion of the smelly camel that reminded her of a boat moving in smooth seas, the scorching sand that stretched all the way to a blue horizon...and the incredible sex they'd had in a tent Bear had ordered erected in a secluded oasis. "I felt like an Arab princess."

"My princess. Selena was born exactly nine months later."

Those had been good times, times when they'd worked together to re-create the villa the Iraqis had destroyed, years when Shana and Bear had been wound up totally in each other, in making a life together that bridged their very different worlds. "Sometimes I wish we could go back..."

As though he sensed her sadness, Bear hugged her before touching the reins and setting the golden horse in motion. "We cannot go back, *houri*, only forward. But it can be just as good. Better."

"Can it?" Shana wasn't at all certain of that. She'd honestly tried to become part of the *Mina Su'ud* community. Though she'd known almost from the first that her efforts would prove futile, she'd labored to master Arabic well enough so she could understand the dialect of the local people and at least carry on a rudimentary conversation with them. It did precious little good that she'd managed to learn to read and write the difficult language almost as well as Bear. "As much as I love the villa, I feel isolated there, especially when you're away. If I could talk with people, understand…"

"I'm not gone all that often." He paused, as if considering what she'd said. "Would it help if we hired all English-speaking help?"

"That would only make people resent me more. And, Bear, you were away from *Mina Su'ud* for at least three weeks of the last month before I left." She turned, took in the genuinely surprised expression on his handsome face. "You didn't even think about that, did you?"

"By Allah, I'm sorry. I should have taken you to Kuwait City where you would have had my mother to keep you company. Would you like to move there?"

"No. There's not a whole lot of difference between being there than at the villa, except that some of the people there speak English and can tell me all about what mission you've gone off on this time that may well leave me a widow."

"I will not die. Do you not believe me when I tell you I've too much to live for to take unnecessary risks?" His voice, though low, rang with conviction.

But his confidence wasn't enough. For ten years Shana had witnessed Bear's anguish, tried to assuage his guilt for having come out of the Gulf War unscathed while Jamil and Asad had been captured. Guilt she knew but could never persuade him was misplaced. For much of that time she had lived in fear that his sense of responsibility toward his countrymen would someday get him killed, and since political tensions had grown worse between Kuwait and its hostile neighbor to the north, her fear had grown to the point she could barely function whenever Bear left on another futile search. "I believe you think you're invincible, but you aren't," she said sadly.

"I have never placed myself in any real danger."

Before Shana could argue the point or even remind him of the serious gunshot wound one of his companions had suffered on a recent excursion into the desert, Bear shifted in the saddle and flicked the reins, and they turned away from the bright morning sun toward a grassy clearing surrounded by ancient oaks. The rushing water of a fast-moving stream whispered softly as it moved over a makeshift waterfall of river rocks caught up on a fallen tree limb.

It was a beautiful setting, reminding her that he was at least trying to show her he valued her, that he was spending his time with her now. She laid her hand over his at her waist, stroking, wishing they could just leave it behind for now, just be Bear and Shana. After a moment, as if he sensed where her mind was going, his hand turned, caressed her, his body becoming less tense behind her.

He stopped at the water's edge, dismounted...reached up to help her down. But his hands lingered at her waist, caressing her hips, and his dark eyes were on her lips, her throat, coursing downward, making her pussy begin to twitch treacherously.

"Let's have breakfast," he said, smiling as he lifted Shana off the horse and set her down. He took a checkered cloth from the basket and laid it out under moss-draped branches of one of the trees. "Sit down, my love, and let me serve you."

How could she love him still? How could she not, when he took such pains to get back into her good graces?

His motions uncharacteristically hesitant, probably because he rarely performed such mundane tasks as unwrapping food and setting tables, he set out their breakfast while she sat cross-legged on the edge of the cloth and waited. She expected him to hand her a plate, but instead he sat beside her, picked up a bunch of fat black grapes and dangled them by their stem.

"You intend to feed me?"

"Yes. Open up." When she did, Bear laid a grape on her tongue.

Its sweet-tart flavor burst in her mouth when she bit into it. "Mmm. Good." So was the service, for he kept on feeding her until the grapes were gone. "You need to eat, too," she told him after swallowing the last one.

"I intend to feast on you."

"Don't you think you'll need your strength for that?" Shana should have objected—after all, they needed to talk about their differences. Sex hadn't caused their rift, and no matter how hot the sex got between them, sex wouldn't heal it. She couldn't make herself protest, though, not when her pussy was already wet from no more than his nearness on the ride out here. Instead she wet her lips with her tongue, anticipating... "I think it's my turn to feast on you," she said, deliberately settling her gaze on the bulge below his tooled leather belt. "I've never feasted on a cowboy before."

Bear grinned. "I'm glad to hear that. Let us both feast on these breakfast sandwiches while we call our daughters. That way we will have fuel in our bodies for all the pleasurable things I have in mind for later."

Shana couldn't say no. In spite of her loneliness and fear, she still loved her husband with all her heart...as well as with her body that even now ached with need, not just for any man, but for him. She couldn't help hoping they could work things out—that he could persuade her they had a future—not only in their shared desire but also in mutual respect and consideration.

A warm breeze fanned them as they finished eating, its effect cooling, soothing, ruffling Bear's wavy hair, tossing a wayward strand across his forehead. Shana watched a bead of sweat make its way down his muscular neck and disappear beyond the opened snap on his red, checkered, western-style shirt. This was a peaceful setting, Shana thought, perfect for her realization that she couldn't seriously fault her husband on any level. Yes, he was stubborn, as tenacious as a rodeo bull bent on tossing off his rider when he set out after something he wanted, believed in.

If he hadn't been so hardheaded, we never would have gotten together. Shana had seen how fiercely he'd had to fight to persuade his father and her own family that they were destined for each other in spite of the obvious roadblocks of different cultures, different religions—hell, their ancestors had been enemies for a thousand years or more. But he'd succeeded. Not only that, but he'd done it in a way that left them both close, not only with their own parents, but with each other's.

After the Gulf War ended, Bear had worked tirelessly to restore burning oil wells to production and keep his family's company solvent. At the same time he'd ignored those who'd said rebuilding the ancient house at *Mina Su'ud* was a fool's task. He'd fulfilled her wishes and built their home on the ruins of the villa where they'd played out her youthful fantasy—and he'd kept his promise that they'd move in before Selena's birth.

Shana had met many powerful men motivated by greed, but Bear wasn't one of them. Pride and honor drove him...that and genuine heartfelt love for his countrymen, his family and friends. Honesty forced her to admit she and their daughters were among the most important of those for whom Bear was driven to protect and defend.

The anger she'd fought so hard to maintain disappeared when she listened to him tease the girls over the phone. It made her feel guilty, for she understood what it was to love an important man, and yet she needed to know she was important, too. She hadn't started to doubt it, ever, until the past couple of years. Maybe she needed to do some changing, too.

My daughters love him, too. How can I deprive them of their dad? Bottom line was, she couldn't. But if Shana was going to go back to him, she had to know he'd at least try to change—to put nourishing their marriage up there with every other duty that had been sapping his time and energy for so long.

Bear set down the cell phone and cleared the remnants of their breakfast off the tablecloth. Then he shot her the predatory grin that had melted her when they'd met for the first time—that still set her skin to tingling...made her anticipate his touch, the feel of his hot breath on her earlobe, her throat, her breasts. Her pussy grew damp, and her pulse raced when she looked into his dark eyes and recognized intense desire—desire she shared. "Come here, my love, I'm ready for dessert."

It seemed he was putting her primary need first—at least for now. "So am I, cowboy. So am I."

* * * * *

Convenient, these zippers that opened the crotches of their jeans. Not as convenient as the more familiar Arab robes—yet more so than conventionally made pants. He'd have to have a few pairs—his and hers—shipped home for times when they wanted to replay this arousing scene. Meanwhile he sucked in a big breath of the fresh breeze that caressed his naked cock and balls as soon as Shana had set them free.

Dahoud found her wet, swollen cunt with his fingers at the same moment she wrapped a dainty hand around his aching cock. He'd missed the incredible pleasure of her caresses last night because he'd bound her. Now he reveled in her arousing touch, the feel of her damp, warm breath when she bent her head to taste him. When she sucked his cock head into her mouth he very nearly came.

Strange yet incredibly arousing, the sensation of them fully clothed but for their exposed genitalia. Stranger, the feeling of exposure—of a gentle breeze tickling flesh unused to its kiss. Sounds of rushing water tumbling over the rocky bed of the waterfall reminded him they might at any moment have company for their tryst. Knowing their privacy might be invaded excited him, made him even harder. It had been a long time—much too long—since he'd taken time to set a scene for seduction, whether in the desert, on the beach, or in some totally new place like this. Dahoud raised his head, nipped Shana's pouting clit.

Her familiar smell—the aroma of a woman in heat—filled his nostrils, made him grasp her rounded ass and position her over his face. Her pussy felt soft, silky, delectable, the plump outer lips already dewy and glistening with her honey. Her little shudder—and the tightening suction of her mouth on his cock when he traced along her slit with his tongue—made him wild, desperate to give and take the ultimate pleasure in the joining.

His balls tightened. His cock twitched. Every muscle in his body tensed when she took him deep down her throat. The more radical of his faith might fantasize about dying martyrs and being met in heaven by sixty virgins, but Dahoud wanted his pleasure here on earth. All he needed was this. His beautiful Shana, pleasuring him. Loving him while he loved her back. Standing beside him now and always.

He stabbed her creamy cunt with his tongue, over and over, loving the way her moans sent streams of erotic vibrations through his cock. Allah, but he wasn't going to be able to hold out much longer.

He closed his mouth over her clit, worried the tight bud between his teeth. When he felt her starting to come, he sucked harder. Had to hurry. Pressure was building low in his torso, painful in its intensity. When she let out a little cry that reverberated against his cock, he exploded. Each of her swallowing motions intensified the feelings, kept him coming in great bursts of satisfaction until he collapsed against their grassy bed. Drained. Spent.

But not satisfied. Dahoud would never be satisfied until he knew he had Shana, not just in his bed and in his home. He'd only rest when he was certain he was firmly back in her heart.

* * * * *

An hour or so later, Shana started to zip her jeans in preparation for the rest of their outing. She stilled her hands, though, when she looked over at the grazing palomino and considered the size of that saddle. She'd always wondered…

Those sex scenes on horseback that she'd read about in romance novels had struck her as addressing the far-out side of female fantasies in terms of possibilities. The arousing scenes hadn't been ones she'd have wanted to risk life and limb to try out in the flesh. But—her pussy clenched with anticipation, aching for him to fill her again, no matter that they'd just made love.

He came up behind her, gathered her in his arms. "What is my *houri* thinking about so seriously?

She smiled, rubbed her backside idly against him. "You. That horse. Bear, could we—"

As her unspoken thought registered in his brain, his cock hardened against her ass and his grip on her body tightened. "Fuck on the back of that horse?" He asked it low, husky, nudging her head to the side as he spoke to nibble her neck, a light touch that sent sensation coursing through her and made her shiver. "You think I should make you ride my cock while we ride him together? I don't see why not. The stablemaster said he was perfectly tame. And he mentioned the saddle was made for two." He shot her a feral grin—a grin full of all sorts of deliciously nasty possibilities. "Want to do it, my kinky little *houri*?"

"Let's." Now wasn't the time for the long, serious talk she'd promised herself they had to have. Not when her whole body tingled with anticipation. She stood and he scrambled to his feet as well, catching her at the waist and practically dragging her to the spot by the stream where he'd tethered the horse.

His hands still at her waist, he paused and directed her attention to the saddle. "I'll mount first then lift you up. I want you facing me so I can see your beautiful face while I fuck you."

By the time Bear settled in the saddle, his exposed cock was hard—more than ready to impale her. Lubrication glistened at the tip of its plum-shaped head, made her mouth water impatiently. Shana put a booted foot backward in the stirrup and held out her hand so Bear could swing her up into the saddle. Her heart pounded in her chest when he lifted first one of her legs and then the other over his own denim-clad, rock-hard thighs, and slowly lowered her onto his rigid flesh.

Oooh. He felt so good, stretching and filling her. Enveloping her in his strength as he worked the reins, setting the Palomino in motion. With each clomp of the horse's hooves, the horn of the saddle cradled at the crack of her buttocks, insinuating itself more deeply until it pressed against her rim, making her writhe and clamp down harder on Bear's hard cock inside her cunt.

"You are in need of release, my *houri*," he told her, his tone teasing. She knew he felt her reaction to the dual sensation and was spurred by it himself, from the almost desperate way he gripped her, the fire in his dark eyes. "You still fantasize about me filling you there, don't you? Putting you on your hands and knees and putting my cock in your ass."

"Yes." She wanted him to fill her there—fulfill a long-held fantasy he'd always refused to bring to life. Yes, she feared it too. Feared he'd split her apart if he put his huge cock in her tight rear passage. It didn't matter. She wanted to experience it all, every expression of desire, of being possessed by the man she'd dreamed of for her whole life, until he'd materialized and made her every dream come true.

His arms surrounded her, bound her to him. Safe…safe from everything but the fear that she might lose him. *Fool. Better to love him now and risk losing him later than to push him away because you're afraid.* "You know I love you," she said softly, cupping his jaw with both her hands.

He leaned closer, gripped her harder. "Then don't leave me again. Trust that I will always come home to you. To this." He shifted in the saddle, driving deeper yet into her welcoming pussy. "I did not sleep for the long days we were apart. For that I must punish you."

Shana shivered at the half-serious expression in his dark, expressive eyes. "Punish me?"

"Later." With a flick of the reins, he brought the horse to a stop and grasped her at the waist. "Now I have an urgent need to fuck you. Claim you again, as thoroughly as if you actually had shut me out of your life."

Oh God. How could she ever have left him? No other man could fill her so completely, bring on these incredible sensations… God help her, she was coming again. She held onto his upper arms, reveling in the strength there in bulging muscles when he lifted her at the waist then slammed her down on his big cock all the way to his satiny ball sac. Again and again, unrelenting, over and over as waves of ecstasy poured through her veins, left her nerve endings thrumming with the intensity of her climax.

When she collapsed against him, exhausted, he let go of his iron control, growling out his own triumph as he came. As burst after burst of his hot come bathed her womb, reviving her own spent desire.

Chapter Five

Fulfill her every fantasy. Every desire she's ever shared with you. Those words resounded in Dahoud's mind late that afternoon after they'd come back to their room...after he'd stripped Shana naked and tied her up in the center of the big bed with silk scarves and slip knots that were more symbolic than serious deterrents to her escape. Even with the low hum of the vibrator he'd inserted in her pussy, she'd quickly drifted off into much-needed sleep. For the third time in ten minutes, he checked the video, thinking how convenient it was that the hotel had provided this handheld monitor so he could leave the room and still check on her regularly.

Allah, but she stirred him in every way, even more now than she had when they'd been hardly more than children. He glanced at the small screen, taking in the tumble of sable curls against the pillow, the curve of her slender throat, her belly with its sapphire jewel, still as firm now as it had been before she'd borne his children. He couldn't keep looking or he'd embarrass himself.

Self-conscious as he perused the array of toys in the hotel's gift shop, he selected a set of butt plugs. If she wanted... Hell, he'd resisted it for ten years for fear of causing her pain, even though the idea of penetrating her anally aroused him, stoked his desire to dominate her... Making up his mind, he pushed the plugs toward the clerk who regrettably was a female who reminded him slightly of his mother. "I will take these, and a package of lubricated condoms."

"Then you'll need some of this, too, won't you?" the woman asked, a smile on her lips and a knowing twinkle in her eye. She held up a tube of lubricant between her thumb and forefinger. "We've got more expensive stuff—flavored, laced with aphrodisiacs, scented, you name it. For my money, though, this is the best. Slick and cool and soothing, if you know what I mean."

Dahoud knew. His cock throbbed under tight denim at the prospect of sinking into his wife's incredibly tight ass... "All right, I will take a tube of that, as well."

"Could I interest you in a collar...some leather goods? A flogger, perhaps?"

He shook his head. Shana had never mentioned wanting to have her satiny skin marked by a whip in the name of sexual satisfaction. He didn't find the idea of doing it particularly exciting, either. The collar, he'd already taken care of. A slender choker of sapphires and diamonds set in platinum lay in the luggage he'd left back at the Houston condo, waiting for his wife to say she'd come home—back to him. "Just these things. And two male submissives. I will need them to come to my rooms later this evening, say around nine o'clock." Hopefully for a very few minutes. If it took longer than that to fulfill Shana's fantasy about being pleasured by more than just him, he might not be able to stem his possessiveness long enough to carry through with it.

He didn't know which would be harder, initiating his wife to anal sex even though he was afraid it would cause her pain—or allowing another male to lay hands or any of his other body parts on the woman he loved. Dahoud scribbled his name on the bill and took the bag the clerk handed to him.

By Allah, the idea of sharing his woman with another man went against the grain. He'd reconciled it in his head, reminded himself Shana had shared him briefly with not one but two hired *houris* years ago. But not in his heart. No. He paused outside the gift shop, looked across the ranch yard toward the distant hills. Familiar country, reminiscent of trips home with friends when he'd attended college in Austin. Different from the land of vast deserts that was his home, yet as awe-inspiring in its own way.

He'd spent long enough here to have adopted a western attitude toward women's rights. No matter how he tried, though, Dahoud couldn't squelch the fury that rose in him when he thought of allowing another man…

He had to. He'd sworn to himself that he'd do whatever it took to get Shana back. Everything except abandon his search for Jamil and Asad. When paper crackled in his hand, he realized he'd clenched his fists—both of them.

If only he could drag her away, as he'd done years ago at her own request, lock her away in his harem as he'd locked her in his heart, wrap her in all-encompassing *abayas* and veils the way his Saudi neighbors still protected their women…

But he could not. He'd married an American woman, agreed to live by western rules in their shared world. Turning from the breathtaking view of the nearby hill country, Dahoud headed for his room, drawn by the presence of the only woman who could give him back his happiness.

* * * * *

Shana stretched, loving the slight soreness that reminded her she'd been well and truly fucked. The light restraints on her wrists and ankles gave her plenty of room to wiggle yet reminded her she was under a man's dominance—Bear's. The fucking swing loomed within easy view of the bed, as did the St. Andrew's cross where she'd been stretched out last night.

Her pussy creamed at the memory of Bear licking her clit and tongue-fucking her pussy while she lay helpless to the delicious onslaught of sensation. Remembering how they'd fucked on horseback earlier this afternoon got her even hotter. There was much to be said for slavery if this was it!

The door opened, and Bear walked in. Damn, but he still looked as good as he had more than ten years earlier when he'd strolled into her brother's hospital room...into her life. Good enough to eat, and she could hardly wait. Her sheikh. Love of her life. Father of her children—and master of her libido.

"Ah, good. You are awake."

How could she not be when his aura filled the room? The sound of his voice, so compelling, so suggestive of hot sex and sensual delights, the enticing smell of his aftershave—the same sandalwood variety he'd used ever since she'd known him—the sight of him looking down at her, a hot, possessive look in his dark eyes... All her senses collided with the stimulus of his presence. "Awake and ready, my master. Ready for anything you may have in mind." She couldn't help the fact that she sounded so breathless—so needy.

He advanced toward the bed, put his hands to his shirt and in one powerful move simply ripped it off, too impatient to bother with the snaps. His gaze locked with hers, conveyed a fierce hunger. Her tongue touched her lips when his hands went to his belt, a gesture that held his attention, made him slow his pace. He took his time now, seemingly aware of how it teased her to watch him slide the belt slowly through its loops, to see him use his fingers to unfasten the jeans, first one button then the next.

"I intend to suck you, fuck you. Possess you. Repeatedly. I will take you in every way a man can take a woman..." As though starved, he kicked away his boots, ripped off his pants and stood naked before her, his huge cock rising proudly from his smooth, tanned groin. God help her, she wanted his muscular arms around her, holding her as though he'd never let her go. She needed his hard body on her, his cock sunk inside her to his satin-smooth balls, his weight pressing her into the mattress. Claiming her for his own, for all time.

She would become an empty husk, devoid of life and spirit if fate ever took him from her. Though she bit her lip to hold back the words, they spilled out, a pathetic entreaty. "Tell me you'll never leave me."

"I will gladly promise to gift you with your weight in precious jewels…make your every fantasy come true. Were it possible I would promise to stay with you always, even throughout eternity." He sat beside her, stroked along the length of her needy body, settling his fingers on an aching nipple. "I am not Allah, and only He may see into the future. Believe that I would move the moon and stars for you if I were able, if only I could ensure that fate would never part us. Believe I will never leave you willingly."

Bear's earnest tone and gentle touch conveyed even more than the words that sounded as though he'd dragged them from deep in his soul. Shame washed over Shana. She should not have asked him for a promise no honest man could make. "Promise, then, that you'll make my every fantasy come true. Make me want you more than I fear losing you."

"It will be my pleasure." Dipping his head, he took her mouth, claimed it with his tongue. His smooth, massive chest brushed her nipples, turned them to rigid shards of sensation. Her desire for her husband fought the fear that had driven her to leave him—and the wanting triumphed. Shana stowed her worry into a far corner of her mind and opened to him—not just her body but her heart. She strained against the light bonds that held her, wanting to touch him, feel satin skin over steel sinew. Wanting to cling to him and pleasure him as he was pleasuring her.

As though she'd voiced her wishes aloud, Bear broke the kiss and freed her. "I want to feel you touching me."

Just as she wanted to embrace him, use her fingers to explore every inch of his magnificent body. Shana held up her arms, wrapped them around Bear's waist when he came down on her, claimed her lips again and tongue-fucked her mouth as though he wanted to devour her. Maybe he did.

His cock throbbed against her inner thigh. She wanted to feel it fill her, stretching her wet, needy pussy, driving away the cold and the fear. She wanted to take every spurt of his hot seed and nurture it...

She needed it now. When she arched her hips, tried to bring her pussy in line with the damp tip of his cock, he resisted. "Later, my greedy *houri*. First, I demand you tell me the fantasies you wish me to fulfill."

Shana sank her fingers into his silky hair, brought his lips back down, close to hers. "I want you to take me every way it's possible for a man to claim a woman. I want to feel your big, beautiful cock in my ass—I've wanted this for years." She'd begged before, when he'd teased her, sliding a lubricated finger along her slit, dipping it in her rear passage just enough to make her want more. "Please."

"Your wish is my command. First, though, you must tell me what else you want. What you whispered about that night last summer when we fucked on the shore of the *Khalij*."

The threesome. She'd never intended to voice that fantasy, but when it had slipped out it had seemed to excite Bear, too. "If you would allow it, I'd like to learn if having two men use me while you watched would excite me." Shana glanced over at the fucking stand, imagined...

"You will experience that, for as long as I can bear seeing another male touching what is mine. Later, however." Bear slid a hand between her legs and ringed her anus with one finger. "Now I will prepare you to take me here, and pray to Allah that I will not hurt you. Raise your knees and open to me."

The only way Bear could hurt her was to go off and get himself killed, but she wouldn't say it, not now when he'd started working the lubricated plug inside her rear passage, all the time rubbing his thumb across the sensitized nub of her clit. God, but she loved the way he did foreplay, starting easy, building her to a crescendo of sexual desire like a conductor might direct a symphony.

She loved feeling his fingers, smooth yet with just enough toughness to remind her he didn't spend all his days laboring over paperwork in his corner office, touching all her erogenous places with exquisite gentleness, yet with all the sureness of a man who knew exactly what he was doing. And the reality of him filling her rear passage, stretching her for his possession, filled her with new sensations — sensations she'd only dreamed about before. "That feels so — incredible. Better than I'd expected it would," she told him when he withdrew the plug and replaced it with a larger one. "It makes me want to come."

"Relax. You will not make me hurry this."

"All right. Master." The new plug stretched her, causing the same sort of pleasure-pain she'd read about in many of the erotic romances she smuggled back home every time she traveled on one of Bear's company planes. Good thing the customs people didn't bother to search luggage when people arrived on private planes owned by Kuwaiti citizens. She loved the feeling of fullness, loved the feel of Bear's big hands stroking her ass cheeks, spreading them. The heat of his fingers probing, sinking into her sopping pussy, sent tingling sensations that started there and spread to her ass, then sped throughout her body.

"Do not come. I've just begun." He slid the plug in and out, slowly, rhythmically, building her need to a fever pitch before taking it out and replacing it once more, this time with one that stretched her almost painfully even with the first, smallest section. "Relax. If you can take this one, you should be able to take my cock. You know you want it. You've wanted it for years, teased me by begging for it."

Maybe she'd been wrong. Her ass burned from this invasion, so much it almost—not quite—distracted her from the urgent need to be taken, to surrender the last vestige of her innocence to her love. Her Master. "Please," she whimpered, not sure whether she wanted him to stop or get on with it.

"Please what?" He bent, sucked first one aching nipple then the other into the warm cavern of his mouth. At the same time he finger-fucked her needy pussy, the motion jiggling the plug in her rectum, intensifying the sensation there.

The heat of his big body seared her. Made her want it all, the pain as well as the exquisite pleasure he promised with every touch, every suggestive thrust of his hard, smooth cock against her inner thigh. "Please fuck my ass. Claim me there as you've claimed the rest of me."

When he withdrew the plug and rolled her onto her stomach she nearly stopped breathing. "Oh God yes, do it," she begged when he positioned pillows under her hips and squeezed out more lubricant in her and on himself. She held her breath again when he rubbed the huge head of his throbbing cock against the entrance to her virgin ass. "Fuck me now!"

"With pleasure." She heard him rip open a packet, felt the coolness of the lubricated condom as he rolled it onto his erection. "You will tell me if I hurt you." Slowly he pressed inward, his cock head breaching the barrier of her tight anal sphincter, the long thick shaft filling her little by little until the smooth, soft skin of his scrotum caressed her wet, hot slit.

She'd never felt so full. So taken. So like the love slave she'd yearned to be in her fantasies—the slave she'd quickly become to her hot-blooded sheikh so long ago. Shana clamped down on her lower lip, resisted the need to beg Bear to fill all of her—to use not only his cock but his hands, his mouth, his body. Pressure built in her pussy with each thrust he made into her ass, and when he slid a hand under her and ran his fingers over her clit she came in huge waves of sensation that left her limp and panting by the time he reached his own climax.

"I love you," she whispered against his thick, tanned neck when she regained her voice after he'd pulled away and gathered her in his arms. "Thank you."

"Believe me, it was my pleasure. Loving you is always my pleasure." He glanced over her shoulder at the watch he hadn't bothered to take off. "In less than an hour, my darling, I will show you I love you more."

Shana's heart beat faster. Did he mean...could he have arranged for the threesome she'd fantasized about so many times while they'd made love? "Bear?"

"Be silent, my curious love slave, and rest. For now I need just to hold you, remind myself you are mine. Only mine."

Chapter Six

Only mine. He'd growled it, the words resonating from deep in his massive chest. His expression had been fierce. Almost frightening in its intensity. Now Shana lay on the bed, pretending to sleep, watching Bear move about the luxurious dungeon.

He stopped and stared for the longest time at the spanking bench before crossing the room and tinkering with the adjustments on the chrome-and-leather fucking swing. Watching him prepare, imagining herself suspended there helpless to his every whim had her pussy twitching, begging to be filled with his magnificent cock. Even now, after a third climax within the past eight hours, it was half-hard, as though the slightest stimulation would bring it to a state of rampant readiness. His balls swung enticingly in their satin-smooth sac, inviting…

Her mouth watered as he moved about, obviously setting a scene for her seduction, lighting candles all around the room. Fat candles, skinny candles, pillar candles on raised stands and tapers in multi-branched candelabra. The exotic scents of tropical fruit and Oriental spices swirled in the breeze when he opened a window and peered outside.

She wanted him so damn much. Not just now but always. Moisture pooled between her legs, and her nipples tingled for the touch of his fingers, his thin but sensual lips, his strong teeth and agile tongue. If only there were two or three of him! She'd made that wish in the height of passion and thought it many other times when she dared not to voice the fantasy. He'd apparently seen it as an indication of deficiency on his part—not the ultimate compliment she had intended. She'd meant she sometimes wished there were more than one Bear loving her, not just any collection of multiple men seeing to her pleasure.

But now that he'd apparently decided to give her what he thought her fantasy was, she was imagining it, imagining men pleasuring her while he watched, getting her body heated and roused for him, prepared to take his cock...

He tinkered with the swing's supple-looking leather seat, adjusting the height then stepping back, only to return and fine-tune it. Shana pictured herself on it, her head hanging at just the right angle for him to fuck her mouth, her ass at the perfect height for him to stand and fuck her there while another lover lay on a bench beneath her, his cock buried balls-deep in her cunt. Her pussy clenched at the imaginary scene.

A knock on the door brought her out of her erotic illusion. The sound also put a scowl on Bear's hawk-like face. He hesitated as though unsure he wanted to admit the intruder, before gritting his teeth and swinging the door open to...

Two hot young studs who dropped matching white terry robes with a flourish and stood before them unashamedly naked, their identical poses reminiscent of ones she'd seen bodybuilders strike onstage at competitions. Neither of them could have been much over twenty, if that. As tall as Bear, they had yet to fill out with any semblance of the massive muscular development Bear had possessed as a UT star linebacker when they'd first met. Shana noticed the blond boys' cocks, long yet not very thick, lying dormant against smoothly shaved groins, the silver rings that passed through both pale heads catching the flickering candlelight.

The boys—neither or both of them—could match her husband. No way. Their downcast eyes hinted they would follow, not lead. No doubt Bear would dominate them as well as her. That thought made her pulse race, and when she assessed her would-be lovers again, she saw them as adjuncts to Bear. Four more hands, two more mouths, two cocks for him to direct in order to enhance her pleasure. A shiver of anticipation coursed through her body when Bear strode to the bed and scooped her up in his arms.

Adrenaline coursed through her veins. Anticipating an all-out assault on her senses from all directions had her honey flowing, dampening her thighs. Her pulse raced, physical manifestation of her runaway emotions as her husband draped her over the seat of the swing, arranged her to his liking and secured her with supple leather straps that held her body motionless, her arms and legs outstretched, her head at an angle that provided easy access for a cock to invade the deepest recesses of her throat. All her erogenous spots lay open, waiting impatiently for a hand or mouth or cock to claim them.

Waiting for the word from Bear, who stood surveying the scene, a scowl on his handsome face as he turned to the two silent studs. "Get on with it. Give my wife pleasure."

Shana lay helpless, waiting, her pussy clenching wildly in anticipation of a delicious onslaught of sensation. The rent-a-studs stood unmoving, as though their feet were glued to the highly polished hardwood floor. Waiting. Waiting for Bear to call "Action" and get this sexual ménage underway.

* * * * *

He couldn't do it. Dahoud's cock felt as though it would burst. The idea of providing Shana with the consummation of a fantasy she'd voiced in the height of passion many times had often gotten him incredibly aroused.

That arousal he'd felt, thinking about this scene, dissipated before the reality. He didn't want these studs touching his wife. He didn't want anybody but him laying a finger on her.

His body was ready. It was his mind he had to whip into submission. He had to reassure himself that the pretty-boy handsome, All-American-type boys who stood before him were not his rivals, were nothing but hired gigolos whose only purpose here was to do his bidding.

Dahoud didn't like the gleam in the taller guy's eyes when he looked at Shana. It reminded him too damn much of the look he'd glimpsed in the mirror of his own expression—needy, incredibly hot and wanting. Still…

Get this over with. Delaying will do nothing to make it easier. He moved over to the fucking swing, laid one palm flat on his wife's creamy ass cheek. "Do not just stand there. Come here. I am giving you permission to touch my wife—I order you to bring her pleasure." He clenched his free hand into a fist at his side. He couldn't help wanting to kill the two when they did his bidding and began a sensual assault on her slender feet before skimming the length of her calves.

When she squirmed a little and whimpered at the dual onslaught, Dahoud almost called a halt. The gigolos had made a fast journey—too fast, as now one ducked under the swing and took her rigid little clit between his teeth while the other bent and ringed her newly initiated asshole with his tongue. *This means nothing. These men are strangers. Think of them as pairs of hands, mouths…instruments of pleasure, same as the dildos and butt plugs.*

Then why can't what they're doing to Shana turn me on? Dahoud forced himself to watch the two men's smoothly choreographed onslaught, felt his cock begin to stir despite the bone-deep fury that they were encroaching on his wife's body—the body that had belonged solely to him, would always belong to him no matter how she might think she wanted to break away.

It didn't matter that he had arranged for this, paid for it the same way he might buy a new bauble to make Shana's eyes light up with pleasure. Still he found the sight of them feasting on the glistening slit he knew so well arousing. Surprisingly so. The tensing of Shana's muscles, the heating of the flesh beneath his hand told him the attention aroused her, too.

He had to be part of it—had to be part of the once-in-a-lifetime experience she'd wanted for so long. Moving to the other end of the swing, Dahoud bent, caught her head between his hands and placed a series of soft kisses along her soft pink lips. "Take me in your mouth now," he ordered, straightening and positioning his cock where his lips had just been. "Are you imagining how it will feel to have three cocks pleasuring you, sucking and fucking you to climax?"

"Oh, yesss." He didn't like hearing the moan of ecstasy that followed her enthusiastic reply, so he stuffed his cock firmly down her throat and began to move within that tight wet cavern. The feel of her tongue stroking his shaft almost made him forget he wasn't the only one taking pleasure from the woman he loved.

Almost.

He found her breasts, kneaded them gently, played with the hard peaks of her nipples. Closed his eyes. Allah but he could not watch another man fucking Shana. She was his, forever bound to him as tightly as she'd used invisible chains to bind him to her.

"No." He felt her say it against his cock head, opened his eyes as he pulled back and freed her mouth. "Please. I don't want this. I want you. Only you."

Allah be praised! Fury boiled up in Dahoud at the sight of one of the gigolos poised to fuck his wife. Killing fury. He clamped down on his emotions, fought for control. After all, he had hired them. They were doing as he'd bid them do.

"Out. Both of you!" he ground out between clenched teeth. "Now!"

The two wasted no time scrambling for their robes and making a hasty escape. Dahoud took the spot between Shana's legs—his spot, damn it—and rubbed a seeking finger along her glistening slit. "Don't tease me, fuck me. Please," she added as though only now remembering he was Master and she was slave.

He moved into position, rubbed his cock head along the path his finger had just taken. "Who is your Master, *houri*?"

"You. Please give me your big, hard cock." When she strained against her bonds, she managed to seat him barely inside her sopping woman's passage.

He could wait no longer. Grasping her ass cheeks, he rammed his cock in her to the hilt. Her ecstatic moans enflamed him, made him pull almost completely out and slam into her. Harder. Faster. Punishing her for having thought she needed more than this. More than his cock, his mouth, his hands. When she used her inner muscles and clamped down on his cock as though she never wanted to let it go, he slid one hand beneath her, found her rock-hard clit. "Come for me now. I command it," he said, scissoring his fingers around the tiny knot of nerves.

"Oh God yessss. Fuck me."

Her honey flowed now, wetting her more. She squeezed his cock harder each time he withdrew. He wouldn't last much longer. The sucking sound of her cunt taking his cock, the smell of sex that filled his nostrils... Seeing her bound before him, her flesh surrounding his, had him on the edge.

"Yesss. Don't stop. You feel...incredible. I'm coming. Come inside me now. Please."

"I am." Hot bursts of come spurted deep and hard, mingling with her juices, claiming her once again. For now...and for all time. In his mind, he'd proven he would do whatever it took to bring his Shana home. He just wasn't certain he had convinced her.

* * * * *

The first thing Shana felt when she woke up was Bear's big hands, gently soothing the sore spots where her bonds had dug into the tender skin of her inner thighs and upper arms. It had barely registered on her overloaded brain when he'd finally plucked her from the swing and laid her on the bed. When she rolled over toward him, needing him to hold her, she noticed light streaming through the French doors of their room.

"Is it morning?" Time had moved too fast if it was, because they'd be heading back to Houston—to their children, her sister's wedding...and the resumption of strain between herself and Bear that she knew was coming.

"Yes, sleepy one. It seems that satisfying three lovers last night sapped a good portion of your energy."

Satisfying? Shana clearly recalled one thing—that her very possessive husband had sent the two studs packing before they'd done more than warm up for the main event. And that he'd stepped in and proved once more that he didn't need help to bring her to a mind-boggling, bell-ringing climax. Several of them, as a matter of fact. Feeling playful, she ran her fingers down her husband's smooth, muscular chest. "I doubt the others got a lot of satisfaction, but as I remember, you did. You certainly satisfied me."

"I know." That came out as a husky, self-satisfied growl.

"Sure of yourself, aren't you?" He was, and Shana knew it—loved that about him as much as she loved his big heart. "You didn't argue when I asked you to send those guys away."

"Humpf." Rolling onto his back and lifting Shana to rest on top of him, Bear shot her an uncharacteristically self-effacing grin. "At least I managed not to strangle them. I admit it was almost impossible to stand by and watch other men giving pleasure to my wife."

"Jealous? You've no need to be."

"Don't I? Did you not walk out on me less than two weeks ago? Might you not prefer a lapdog who will do your bidding in every way?"

If Shana didn't know better, she'd have thought the moisture at the corner of Bear's eye might be a tear—but that idea was ludicrous. "I might prefer you if you didn't run off risking your precious neck every time someone hints they might have spotted Kuwaiti prisoners in Iraq. Bear, it's been ten years."

"And Jamil might still be alive. I will not abandon him, or Asad, or any of the others. Anything else you ask of me, I will gladly do." He wrapped his arms around her, drew her down until her cheek rested on his chest. "Your body tells me you do not truly want to leave me."

"No, I don't. But the uncertainty..." She'd talked with him about this too many times. He wasn't going to bend, and she didn't know if she could. "I don't know if I can live with it."

"Shana, love. What about your heart? I could not bear it if..." He stopped, breathed deeply. When she tried to look up at his face, she found she could not raise her head because he was holding her neck too firmly. "...I thought I was hurting you." His voice suddenly turned ragged, and she wondered if what she heard choking his throat was sadness. When she finally managed to raise her head, she saw the tears he was rapidly blinking away.

When he regained control, he looked her in the eye. "Life is uncertain, darling. I could be hit by a car on the streets of

Kuwait City—or Houston. Do you want to give this up?" Lifting her at the waist, he lowered her onto his cock. "Last night you said no when another man was about to take you."

No, she didn't want to walk away. And Bear had spoiled her so much that she didn't want anybody but him, fantasies aside. He'd fulfilled her sexual fantasies—even ones he didn't share. By doing so he'd proven to her that many of them were only idle musings, thoughts to titillate and enhance their own love life, not deep-seated desires she longed to experience firsthand. The others, they'd incorporated, shared, enjoyed together as they broadened their sexual horizons.

He flexed his hips, seated himself in her fully. "Shana?"

"I didn't want to be fucked by strangers."

"You would have welcomed a ménage with one or two of our friends?"

"No!" The very idea of sharing physical intimacy like that with men she'd bump into at every turn appalled her.

"Then, my *houri*, you only want me in your bed. You would miss me terribly if I let you go—so I will not." Lifting his head, he took her left nipple in his mouth and suckled, slowly fucking her in long, smooth strokes that had her on the verge of coming.

"I don't know. Oh God, don't stop. You're being unfair." Waves of ecstasy started deep in her belly, undulated through every nerve, each muscle, until she collapsed on his chest, a mass of quivering delight. The hot spurts of his come a few minutes later started her climaxing all over again.

Chapter Seven

"You two must have had an interesting night," their hostess said when Bear and Shana finally made it downstairs to check out. "Was everything satisfactory?"

Bear smiled. "Quite. I'm sure we will be visiting you again."

Shana wasn't sure about that, although the experience had helped her to remember, in a potent way, that there truly was something erotic about being confined for sex — about submitting completely to her lover's desires and trusting him to give her pleasure, not pain. "Could you recommend a place we might get something to eat?" she asked.

"You've missed breakfast here, and lunch won't be for another hour or so. If you're hungry I suggest the Roadhouse Diner. It's about five miles down the road on the right, not too far from the entrance to the interstate."

"Thanks." Maybe the diner would offer a quiet booth — a place to talk where desire couldn't encroach on conversation, or rather where they wouldn't be able to act on anything of that nature that might come up.

A few minutes later they settled side by side in the last empty booth at the diner and chose to share a large plate of homemade tortilla chips dipped in a creamy guacamole concoction that seemed to fascinate Bear. "What is in this?" he asked after piling the last of the stuff onto the last chip.

Shana finished chewing her last bite. "Avocado. Tomatoes. Cilantro. A little onion, I think. And sour cream. I take it you like it?"

"Yes. Will you make it for me back home?"

"I'll make some for you in Houston." Shana still wasn't sure about a long-term reconciliation, but she'd agreed they'd stay together for the days before and during her sister Leah's wedding. "You know, I haven't agreed to go back with you to *Mina Su'ud*."

Bear squeezed her thigh just above the knee, as though reminding her body how it needed him. Damn, it did just that, sending urgent messages to her pussy, her breasts, messages that practically shouted out their need, their mindless desire—for him. "You will," he said, sliding his hand up her leg, cupping her sex through the barrier of her bikini panties. "Your cunt already weeps for me."

Yes, it did. Still she wouldn't give in. "Let's take one day at a time," she said, hating the pleading tone of her voice. "We'd better get going if we're going to make it back to Houston in time to pick up the girls tonight."

* * * * *

That night Dahoud lay awake, long after he and Shana had tucked in their daughters, after they had made love in the familiar surroundings of the condo she had decorated for them years ago in an eclectic mix of East and West. As he watched her sleep, he breathed in fragrant smoke wafting in from the bathing room—sandalwood and jasmine and something else that was unique, like the partnership they had forged.

They had bridged real differences, set aside ancient enmities that still ripped nations asunder and built a home where each of them respected the other's beliefs and customs. He could not allow her concerns about his safety to tear them apart, not when he loved her and knew she returned his love in full measure.

Her long dark hair cascaded over the pillow onto his arm, its strands a silken tether, a point of connection he could not allow to be broken. Not even for his honor. Not even for the possibility of bringing Jamil home unless someone brought him incontrovertible proof of his cousin's whereabouts. Dahoud closed his eyes against the incredible suffering he knew the Iraqi devils visited on their captives, clasped Shana's hand.

She stirred, smiled sleepily at him. A satisfied smile. Dahoud's cock began to stir when she rolled onto her side and wiggled her firm buttocks against him. "You'll never pass a night away from me again," he murmured against her hair.

* * * * *

Enslaved. Enslaved by love. Shana could no more stay away from Bear than she could quit breathing. She didn't want to stay away from him. She'd known it before they'd gone to Leah's wedding this afternoon. Defending her marriage to her sister's Hassidic in-laws had only strengthened her resolve. She had to find a way, a middle road that would allow her to go back home.

Home to *Mina Su'ud*, to the villa on the *Khalij*. Shana had never felt the scorn of the people there, even though she couldn't manage to speak their language. The shopkeepers smiled when she wrote out what she wanted, or proudly called for their youngsters to translate their answers. No one had ever treated her rudely. Even the nomadic Arabs who lived on Bear's land always greeted her with smiles.

Yes, Bear's world had been alien to her at first, still was to some extent, but she felt welcomed there. Not like she'd felt today, having to endure the thinly veiled hostility of some of David's relatives at the wedding reception they'd finally escaped.

Their very different worlds weren't the issue. Had never been, except to the extent her lack of spoken Arabic isolated her from their neighbors. Bear's work wasn't the problem, either. Since Shana was being totally honest with herself, she'd admitted her fear was less that Bear would die than that he'd relegated her and their relationship to somewhere less than first place in his priorities.

And she didn't really believe that. Not now. Not after he'd come halfway around the world to show her how much he loved her. And not after they'd both had to endure the censure of Leah's in-laws for the past five hours.

Shana stepped out of the simple silk sheath that had caused so much comment for its supposed immodesty, and turned to Bear. "I wish I'd have shown up in *hijab*. Or maybe in this." She snatched up a pair of shimmering harem pants and matching bolero and held them up in front of the dressing room mirror.

He hung up his tie and turned her way. "I am sorry if someone made you uncomfortable because of me." His breath warmed her neck when he came up behind her and wrapped his arms around her waist.

"Oh, it's not just us the older women were *kvetching* about. They couldn't believe their precious David was marrying into a family of heathens. Just because we don't wear long sleeves and skirts down to our ankles, or cover our hair the way they do, or spend our whole lives segregated from our men except for—"

"Or stick with your own kind, as I overheard one of the old men saying to Jake. Apparently they consider it a disgrace that Leah's sisters and brother all married outside their faith."

"They'd better not have insulted you." Shana had hated the segregated festivities that had kept her away from her husband and made her worry that one of her new brother-in-law's male relatives would make her Muslim husband feel uncomfortable. "Or Jake or Deb's Scott."

"They seemed equally aghast about me and the Christian husband and wife. I wasn't singled out. The women must have gotten to you badly. I am sorry, my love." Bear slid his hands up her body, clasped them over her breasts, warming her heart as well as her goose-bumped skin.

His touch sent shivers through her. Made her want him to take her, reaffirm his claim to her body, her heart, her soul. "I'm sorry, too. I even felt bad for Alice. David's great-aunt Binnie zeroed in on her like a dive bomber after a prime target."

"We all survived," Bear said mildly. "I imagine Leah and David will not be seeing a lot of his family."

That was probably true, especially since most of them lived in New York City and the newlyweds would be settling in Houston. "Fortunately." Shana said a silent "thank you" for her own loving in-laws. "Let's not talk about this anymore. I want to lie in your arms, feel your heart beating next to mine while we make love."

"For now?"

"No, my darling sheikh. Forever, as long as God grants us life. I want you to take me home."

Epilogue
One year later...

☙

Shana had never looked more beautiful than she did now, holding their two-month-old son in her arms as the sapphires in his collar winked at him from its place around her creamy throat. Dahoud bent to kiss them both but remembered—

"I'm filthy. I need to bathe." The helicopter ride had left him coated with sand churned up by the rotors, sand that clung to the crude that had drenched him when a new well had come in earlier that day. "Jake landed just before I did. He's cleaning up in the guesthouse so he can come meet his new nephew." Though Dahoud had managed to delegate many of his duties, he'd wanted to be on hand today to see the first new well since the war come in on Jamil's land. Somehow, seeing new life spring from the desert gave him new hope that someday he'd find his cousin.

He'd tracked down several more dead-end leads about Jamil and Asad, but he'd made certain never to let Shana and his girls have reason to believe they didn't come first in his heart. Now, though worry creased her brow each time he left on a hunt, she knew she was the only Paradise he would ever seek, his reason for living and fighting to be back to her side no matter what. That knowledge had apparently helped her accept the fear that came with her love for him. The love he treasured and would never take for granted again.

When she'd acknowledged his conflict between desire and duty by deciding to name their son for Jamil, he did not think he could love her more but he did. He hoped Jamil would one day meet his namesake.

* * * * *

Tonight, after he washed up, Dahoud joined her on the balcony of their suite. He could tell she was worrying about her brother. "He will be fine, *houri*."

"I'd like to strangle Alice. If anybody should have children, it's my brother. Our girls adore him, and he's so good with them."

Dahoud laid his hand at her waist. "He will. As you've said many times, he and Alice were ill-matched." He'd said much the same thing earlier to Jake, even though he sensed the pain was too new, too intense for his words to have much if any soothing effect. "We, on the other hand—"

"—are ecstatically happy. You are, aren't you?"

"Never doubt it. I count myself the luckiest man on earth, having you, our girls—and now our fine, healthy son." Dahoud looked out over the water, calm tonight, lit by the stars and the running lights of tankers, red, green and white like the fireflies that lit the courtyard garden. "Jake will find the right woman. I'm certain of it."

Shana turned to him, placed her hands on his shoulders. "I know. Still, I can't help hurting for him. And it makes me furious to think that woman sprung it on him at Cousin Greg's wedding."

"Calm down, *houri*. Your brother needs no one to fight his battles. Come, it's getting late, and I want to show you just how much I love you."

Gently, for Jamil's birth had been difficult, he lifted her, carried her to bed, impaled her. Claimed her again, for all time. She submitted so sweetly and so completely, his love slave.

It struck Dahoud as they lay sated in each other's arms. It was he, the Master, who was enslaved. Forever enslaved by the beautiful woman who had long ago stolen his heart.

Entrapped

ಬ

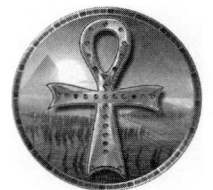

Chapter One
ଛ

At least the American's screams had ceased. For now.

Perhaps for eternity.

Since January 16, 1991 Jamil al Hassan had lain each night on the same filthy cot, chained hand and foot to iron rings imbedded in the rough concrete walls of an underground bunker not far from *al Qurnah*, where the Tigris and Euphrates Rivers converged to form the *Shatt al-Arab*.

The Iraqis had captured him after his fighter took a hit and went down in the midst of a swirling sandstorm over the heavily guarded *Zugayr* oilfield. They'd kept him when they had repatriated many of his countrymen because he'd had the misfortune to have nearly completed his university education in geo-petroleum engineering at a time when the Iraqis desperately needed all the experts they could find to help rebuild their war-ravished oilfields.

His punishment for failing in his mission had been enslavement by the Iraqi dogs who had overrun his homeland. His fate for having been so stupid as to barter for his countrymen's freedom with his expertise in rebuilding ruined oil wells had extended his imprisonment—and his existence on earth—indefinitely. Sometimes—hell, most of the time—he cursed the sense of duty that had been bred into him and which had made him put fellow prisoners' welfare above his own.

Jamil had lost track of dates, but this was the eleventh spring season he'd spent in captivity. That it was spring, he confirmed by the presence of water that dripped from the bunker ceiling onto his naked body—water that came to the

Zubayr Rumaila only when the snows melted and flowed down the Tigris and Euphrates Rivers from the mountains to the north.

Jamil shivered more from grim anticipation of what form his torture would take on the morrow than from the cold, for the bite of frigid north winds rarely traveled this far south.

A plaintive moan caught in the fetid air and drifted to Jamil's ears. The American his captors had brought here recently from a prison somewhere west of Baghdad must have survived his brutal initiation at the hands of chief jailer Mohammed Dubaq and his henchmen.

Apparently the Americans were rumbling loudly of war, of avenging the deaths of thousands of their civilians at the hands of a few fanatic Islamic terrorists. Rumors flew among Jamil's captors that U. S. troops lay in wait with brutal firepower, amassing more men and equipment daily all over the region, including thousands in Kuwait and more in the tiny sheikhdom of Qatar. The jailers grumbled that many American airplanes flew over Iraq every day dropping bombs on antiaircraft defense sites.

Nearly every day Jamil saw white streaks in the sky that he recognized as the trails of jet fighters. Many more of them lately than before. He imagined some of them had taken off from the Prince Sultan Airbase in Saudi Arabia, as he had done eleven years ago on what had proven to be his personal journey into hell.

This new threat to the Butcher of Baghdad brought Jamil hope where there had been none. And now his captors had brought him a potential ally in the American. Unlike his countryman, Asad al Qassimi, who lay near death in the cubicle next to the guard's post, the American might still possess the strength to attempt escape.

"Asad?" he whispered, wanting assurance that his cousin Dahoud's former executive assistant still lived.

The guard stomped to his cell. "Be silent. Your friend yet breathes. If you wish to join him in his pain, disturb my sleep again."

"A thousand apologies," Jamil murmured, not anxious to feel the jailer's boot. At least this wasn't Dubaq, the perverted warden, or one of his favorite accomplices. This man treated guarding prisoners as a job, not an opportunity to visit untold miseries upon his helpless victims.

On occasion Jamil had heard the man mutter about the inhumanity of treatment accorded the prisoners by their captors—and express his disgust at the soldiers and their perverted pleasures.

Jamil didn't even know the man's full name, only that he was called Maktoum, and that he was one of the Marsh Arabs who had lost his nearby home when Hussein had ordered the Marshes drained, leaving the area unfit to support life.

Five nights of every seven, Maktoum guarded the prisoners in this bunker, offering Jamil and Asad—and now the American—blessed respite from the physical and psychological torture meted out by Dubaq and his subordinates on a daily basis.

For what seemed like the forty-thousandth night he lay on the narrow cot, trying to conceive a way of getting word to Dahoud...of obtaining assistance from someone with freedom to move about who would not report him, resulting in the slow, torturous mutilation and death of his fellow prisoners or himself.

His acquiescence and Asad's had bought their countrymen some time and suffering but nothing more. They now lay dead in Dubaq's crude common grave at the edge of the oilfield. But now that time was running out for Asad. For himself, too. Escape, if it was possible, would have to be soon.

But he had to trust someone other than himself to contact his cousin in Kuwait. Someone with freedom to move who would be amenable to betraying his employers for a fistful of Kuwaiti *dinars*.

Maktoum?

The lazy guard's snores rumbled through the bunker.

Jamil dared not approach any of Dubaq's soldiers, and he had no access to the other Marsh Arabs who did menial labor around the encampment.

It would have to be Maktoum. Jamil had little choice but to pray the Marsh Arab's betrayal of his superiors might be bought.

He shifted, trying to find some comfort within the confines of the cot and his chains. There was only so far a man could move with his ankles and wrists shackled to the four corners of the tiny cubicle. A heavy iron collar circling his neck and attached with chains to eyelets above his head further impeded his ability to move.

Bruised and battered from the latest round of beatings Dubaq had administered, Jamil closed his eyes and willed himself to sleep—to elude this living hell for a few blessed hours.

His nightmares came less often now.

But today's round of torture weighed heavily on his mind. This time he'd escaped the humiliation of standing naked before his jailers, being beaten and threatened with branding, castration, and eventual death. Dubaq's fiendish attention had focused instead on Asad, who for the past month had been refusing to work on the oil wells and taunting his captors as though he wished to die. And on the newly arrived American lieutenant, Brian Shearer.

Water dripped through the porous ceiling, stinging the wounds on Jamil's chest that had not yet healed from his latest encounter with the warden's whip.

Asad's anguished screams still rang in Jamil's ears. For ten days now, Dubaq had been hacking off a finger a day. If Dubaq followed his usual pattern, castration would come next, followed by a slow death from the festering wounds. Jamil had observed the jailer's methods of torture well over the past eleven years.

And he knew he'd escaped mutilation so far because his knowledge of the oil wells made him valuable enough for Dubaq to keep him not only alive but reasonably fit for work. A similar knowledge had saved Asad as long as he'd been willing to apply it.

Not that the psychological torture Jamil had endured during the first years of Dubaq's tour as commander of the prison outpost was any less painful. It had taken him years to shut off his mind and accept the inevitable whenever Dubaq had ordered him stripped and shackled to the bunker wall for his perverted games.

At least the rapes had ceased. Jamil supposed Dubaq's woman who had arrived from Baghdad about a year ago was now his victim of choice when he wished to satisfy his carnal urges. Lately, all Jamil had been forced to endure were beatings and stomach-curdling threats of death and dismemberment during the hour or more he spent chained to the bunker wall each day for so-called interrogation.

That and the unrelenting pressure from the ball-stretcher Dubaq had ordered him to wear soon after his arrival.

The jailer had never rescinded that order even after he had ceased the weekly rapes. And Jamil dared not remove it himself for fear of attracting more of Dubaq's unwanted attention to his genitals.

"I will keep tightening it, and when I tighten it sufficiently, the ring will destroy your manhood," Dubaq had said each time he'd squeezed and jerked on Jamil's tortured testicles while ramming his cock up Jamil's ass. "You will be a eunuch. Enjoy the sensations of pleasure while you can, Kuwaiti devil."

A eunuch? Jamil would rather have been dead.

But what did it matter, since he could hardly find pleasure, shackled and enslaved?

His pleasure came only in the freedom within his mind. Only in his dreams.

* * * * *

Grunts and groans filtered through thin walls of the jailer's barracks. Dubaq must be going at her sister-in-law again, despite the advanced state of Mernoosh's pregnancy.

Leila al Sinan shrugged. The sounds coming from Mernoosh's throat bespoke pleasure, not pain, though Leila sometimes thought the two sensations must be closely related.

She'd have been better off completely alone in Baghdad than here, where each day she had to watch Saqr's older sister preen over the fact that she had a husband and Leila did not.

When Mernoosh had persuaded Leila a year ago to come with her to this desolate outpost miles from any form of civilization, she'd promised there would be many handsome young Iraqi soldiers from which Leila might choose a new husband. Instead, the soldiers under Dubaq's command were few, toothless, fat, and ugly—outcasts kept here in this miserable place to guard an oilfield and a handful of Kuwaiti prisoners the government had been holding since its invasion of Kuwait had been thwarted more than ten years earlier.

A handful of prisoners whose numbers had decreased on an almost weekly basis since her arrival.

Mernoosh's husband appeared to be younger than any of his men, and by Leila's reckoning he had to be at least forty years old. Not that she'd have looked twice at Mohammed Dubaq even if he wasn't married to Saqr's sister. Not after having witnessed the bite of his lash and recognizing a streak of sadistic cruelty in him that she guessed he must temper with Mernoosh, who apparently worshiped him.

No. Leila would do without a man if she couldn't attract a more desirable one than the louts who worked with Mernoosh's husband.

Still her *yoni* ached. She yearned for Saqr's touch, though more than a third of her twenty-six years had passed since he'd died fighting for Iraq. Her left cheek ached, too, reminding her she would always bear awful scars. Scars left from burns she had suffered on the heels of learning her young husband's fate, when the Americans had begun their relentless bombing of Baghdad.

Attacks that had left the few remaining members of her family dead.

Mernoosh's whimper brought home the fact that Leila had no one to take care of her carnal needs.

Aroused by the sounds of sex that drifted through walls as thin as paper, she dipped one hand between her legs. Her *yoni* wept, as if mourning the lack of a man to pleasure it.

She ran the fingers of her free hand over the rough, uneven-textured skin on the left side of her face before letting them drift along the scars that stretched across her jaw, her neck, on the outer curve of one breast and down her arm. In the light of day, no man with the gift of sight would look at her with lust in his eyes.

Her pierced nipples had remained undamaged by the flames. They beaded now at the touch of her fingers, just as her clitoris hardened and tingled at her touch.

Mernoosh cried out, the ecstatic sound reminding Leila of the way Saqr used to make her scream with pleasure when she came. Dubaq's lusty yell soon followed.

Leila's *yoni* grew hotter. Moisture gushed onto her hand. Pressure built inside her, so intense she wanted to scream.

Desperate for release, she rubbed her swollen clitoris harder, caught it between her fingers and pinched it hard. But her hand was no longer enough to keep the yearning at bay.

By Allah, the Kuwaitis and their American friends had stolen her husband and her looks. She wouldn't let them steal her life.

She'd take vengeance along with her satisfaction. Now, before Dubaq executed the last of the enemy dogs he'd been keeping alive so he could torture them in that foul-smelling bunker he called a prison.

She'd take her pleasure, steal the seed they'd ripped from Saqr when they blew up the tank he'd been driving through the desert. *Insha'Allah*, that seed would take root in her womb and give her a child to love.

There would be no better time for action than now, before the last of the prisoners succumbed to the release of death.

Only two of the original Kuwaiti prisoners remained — plus the American who had arrived earlier today and endured a vicious "interrogation" by her brother-in-law. He would hardly be fit for fucking even if Leila could stomach the idea of having sex with one of Saqr's killers, and neither would the older Kuwaiti whose last remaining finger Dubaq had boasted about hacking off this afternoon.

That left one—the Kuwaiti oilfield engineer, Jamil al Hassan. The prisoner Dubaq forced to work in the oilfield nearly every day. He had told her his name once, months ago, when she'd delivered his meager midday rations while he supervised some sort of complex-looking repair to a damaged pump.

Her nipples tightened when she pictured his muscles straining while he tightened a valve, the contrast of his olive skin against the white *ghutra* on his head and the endless expanse of pale desert sand...his sensual mouth and large, dark eyes.

Al Hassan seemed a likely specimen.

Leila stopped fingering her wet *yoni*. Quickly she wrapped a black silk *hijab* around her head, more to conceal her scars than to preserve her modesty. The *abaya* and *shaila* would serve dual purposes, as well.

Their blackness would allow her to blend in with the night, and their all-encompassing cover would conceal her identity should she be seen. Maktoum, the night guard, would surely be asleep. If not, she would lurk in the shadows, find her way past him to Jamil.

Her nipples puckered when she moved and the rough homespun fabric of her *abaya* abraded them. Her heart beat faster as she sneaked from Mohammed's house while he and Mernoosh still giggled and groaned in their bed.

Accustomed as she was to lurking in the darkness, Leila had no trouble adjusting her vision to the dim illumination from a naked bulb near the bunker stairway.

Maktoum the guard slept as soundly as she'd guessed he would, his snores resounding off the walls within the bunker's close confines. Water dripped, dripped, dripped from the ceiling to the packed sand floor.

The American groaned intermittently while the older Kuwaiti prisoner lay as still as death on a cot beside the guard. Neither appeared to be shackled. Leila assumed that was because the injuries that had resulted from today's torture made it unlikely that they would attempt escape.

Jamil lay quietly, his legs and arms spread wide and chained to the four corners of his cubicle. His chest rose and fell slowly, regularly. It was good he was bound. She was certain his overweening Kuwaiti pride would never allow him to take her willingly.

She raked him with her gaze, anticipated him giving her the woman's pleasure she had been missing for so long. What male beauty!

And what a shame for it to be confined so cruelly. She shuddered when she noticed the iron collar around his neck. If he attempted to move his head, he would choke to death.

His body, though thin, looked surprisingly fit considering the treatment he had endured. She supposed he had cuts and bruises. It would have been a miracle if he didn't, considering that her sister's husband spent a good part of each day supervising his prisoners' torture. But she didn't see any in the weak light from that one light bulb near the door.

Even in the near darkness she could tell his *lingam* was long and thick, and resting at the moment against his inner thigh. Leila's mouth watered.

She hiked up her *abaya* and straddled him, then rubbed her *yoni* over his sleeping sex. When he opened his eyes, she clamped her hand over his mouth.

"Silence, Kuwaiti dog, or you die now. *Nek ni.*"

Jamil blinked.

Was he dreaming? Had this apparition just demanded in a raspy whisper that he fuck her?

No. This was no apparition, and it wasn't one of Dubaq's cock-sucking underlings. This was a woman. He swelled against what unmistakably was a warm, wet pussy. But all he could see in the dim light was a figure swathed in black, its features obscured but for the whites of dark, inscrutable eyes.

She smelled of greasy roasted goat and yogurt—or was that the stench of his own unwashed body?

Apparently his cock didn't care. Like a man long deprived of water who had suddenly spied an oasis pool, it quickened and sought the opening to paradise.

Its aim unerring, Jamil's cock found its target and sank inside the tight, wet glove of a sleek satiny pussy. His balls strained against the hard leather stretcher, making him bite his tongue to avoid crying out with agony when she began to ride him.

He tried to concentrate on her movements—slow, rocking, almost like that of a camel lumbering across the desert.

"Unchain me," he ordered roughly, suddenly anxious to touch her, to discover if she was real or only another cruel illusion.

"Silence! Lest you feel the sting of my lash," the guard roared, his voice raspy with obvious annoyance at being awakened.

She bent, obscuring the faint light, and whispered near Jamil's ear. "I have no key. Be silent or you will summon the guard."

By Allah! For a moment he'd forgotten his keeper who slept not ten feet from his cell. "If you have a care, at least loosen the leather that binds my testicles. Surely you can feel it." He whispered this time, near where he thought her ear must be.

Her rocking motions ceased. She cupped his tortured balls, found the stretcher. It bit harder into his flesh, then fell away, its sting replaced by the delicious sensation of her callused fingers. Gentle fingers, rubbing away the pain. Caressing his balls as only a woman would.

Her hot, wet sheath, squeezing his cock as only a woman's pussy could.

Jamil lay helpless, deprived of the sight and taste of his phantom lover, able only to feel the touch of her hand on his scrotum and her vagina contracting around his cock. He lay back, savoring the sensual motions of a female body cloaked head-to-toe in all-concealing black.

His nostrils flared at the almost forgotten smells of musk and sex. Her quickened breathing and his own reverberated, their faint sounds mingling with the monotonous drips of falling water droplets in the silence of the bunker.

He had to taste her. Yet he couldn't move, and he dared not ask her to bend down and give him her lips. He dared not chance waking the guard again. He surely would end this fantasy fuck ere it truly began.

Jamil deliberately slowed his breathing, kept it quieter than the constant drip, drip, drip of water onto his legs, arms, and upper chest where she did not shield him with her robe and veil. Quieter than the occasional moans from the American in the cubicle next to his.

His fingers itched to cup her breasts, feel a woman's softness in his hands for the first time since his enslavement. He strained at his bonds. But the chains held fast.

Was she beautiful or ugly? The slight weight of her, balanced as it was above his cock, hinted that she was slender beneath the all-encompassing *abaya*. Beyond that he could tell nothing but that her pussy knew exactly how to clench his long-deprived cock.

It didn't matter. Heat radiated through his body, from his cock that she squeezed and drew on so sweetly, from the sensation of her gentle fingers kneading his balls.

Jamil concentrated on what he could feel, savored each subtle undulation of her vaginal muscles as she moved up and down, taking him deeper and then withdrawing. The tug of her fingers when they tangled in the coarse mat of pubic hair that surrounded his balls—hair he'd not been allowed to remove during his incarceration but whose presence humiliated him now.

Her juices gushed over him, dripped back onto his anus. She caught it on her finger and rubbed it around the puckered opening where Dubaq had violated him so regularly before the women arrived in camp.

Better a woman's finger than a man's cock. Still, being touched there brought back nightmarish memories.

"Not there. Please. *Katha ath nan*," he whispered in Arabic, hoping she would understand and caress his genitals but leave his ass alone. Apparently she did, because she slid her hand up until her nails raked his scrotum and her fingers grasped his testicles painfully as though to remind him who was slave, who was master.

"No. *Nek ni*. Fuck me," he repeated in English, for he realized his command of colloquial Arabic left much to be desired since he'd spent years being schooled in the States before returning to Kuwait to defend his country.

"*Kul khara!*" she hissed, ordering him to shut up while she fondled his sac. At the same time she sank onto his cock again, taking all of him into her pussy this time and clasping him with inner muscles that seemed determined to wring every drop of semen from his tortured balls.

Her grip on his balls became lighter, more sensuous than painful. His control gone, he felt his cock swell further. With each orgasmic spasm of her pussy around him, she sped the inevitable explosion that had him in its grasp.

First, a kaleidoscope of color. Then total blackness. Jamil lay chained, ejaculating his milky semen into the body of a stranger—a woman he'd never touched, never tasted. A woman he'd never heard shout her pleasure, even during the fierce orgasm that had triggered his own release.

A woman who disappeared as suddenly as she'd come, taking the best part of him with her.

Chapter Two

Were it not for the ball stretcher lying between his legs and the dried love-juices he noticed on his cock and balls when the guard unchained him the following morning, Jamil would have dismissed his nocturnal visitor as the prime player in a strange erotic dream.

Surreptitiously, he wiped away the evidence that could earn him a beating or worse and refastened the brutal device lest Dubaq notice its absence and make good on his latest castration threats. Then he pulled a tattered *dishdasha* over his head as though he thought he was to leave immediately to work in the oilfield.

This morning his captors would have to strip him down if they wanted to play.

* * * * *

The prisoner's long, thick cock had more than filled her. It had shot her full of his thick, milky seed while she'd enjoyed an orgasm more intense than any of those embedded in her distant memories.

Jamil al Hassan had fulfilled long pent-up needs that, once Leila had acknowledged them, refused to stay satisfied.

She wanted more. She wanted to stroke his skin, feel his hands and mouth on her cheek, her nipples. Her clitoris. Thinking about how sweetly Saqr used to suckle her *yoni* while she took his *lingam* deep into her throat had her wet and aching again.

Saqr's much less impressive *lingam* had been smooth, hairless.

A thicket of coarse, curly hair had surrounded the prisoner's cock and balls. And an unkempt beard obscured the mouth she soon would have tasting her most tender flesh.

The hair must go.

It was unfitting for a Muslim, which Jamil almost certainly must be. More important, Leila found it distasteful to touch and look upon.

Dubaq might well like the idea of taunting his prisoners with possible dismemberment at a woman's hands. He might even welcome her offer to divest them of their disgusting body hair.

Congratulating herself for coming up with a plan, Leila slipped into one of the high-necked, long-sleeved tunics that hid the ruined flesh on her arm and neck. Very carefully she wrapped a purple silk *hijab* around her head, arranging it to conceal the worst of her facial scars as well as her hair before tucking its ends into the neckline of the tunic.

"Good morning, my sister." Mernoosh looked up from the table where she and Dubaq were feeding each other dates and flatbread. Fragrant steam escaped from a small pot of coffee on the stove.

"Good day," Leila said as she joined them.

When Dubaq grunted after finishing off the last of the dates, Leila seized the opportunity to put her plan in action before he left to attend his duties. "My brother, I would do my part to intimidate our enemies."

His beady eyes glittered. "And what might you do that I cannot?"

"You have threatened to take their manhood, have you not?"

"I plan to take the older Kuwaiti's balls this morning if he yet lives. Stubborn dog. He refuses to die, yet he does nothing to make me wish to allow him to live. He steadfastly refuses to admit his country's crimes against Iraq. He refuses even to assist us in the oilfields now, though he must know his aid there is what has kept him alive all these years. Do not tell me, little sister, that you wish to be the one to make him a eunuch."

"No. That is a pleasure I will gladly leave to you."

Leila suppressed a shudder. Asad, the gaunt Kuwaiti who had apparently decided a fortnight ago that a slow and painful death was preferable to continuing his enslavement, had appeared near death when she'd crept past his cot in the hour before dawn. Obviously he had borne the brunt of her brother-in-law's most recent sadistic torment.

Still, the potential castration of Asad offered her a perfect opportunity. She forced a smile when she met Dubaq's interested gaze. "Allow me to remove the body hair from all three prisoners while you and your men assure them that one of them is about to lose his balls," she said, taking care to sound casual. "I would make the experience suitably painful in payment for what they did to Saqr."

Mernoosh, who Leila was beginning to believe possessed a sadistic streak to match her husband's, clapped her hands. "Mohammed. I beg you allow my brother's widow her vengeance."

"I will, my jewel. But I would take it further."

Dubaq's evil smile chilled Leila's heart. What if he decided to castrate all three men? Her *yoni* clenched at the thought of never having Jamil's magnificent cock inside her again. Her mouth turned dry when she imagined it soft and flaccid against her tongue, unable to harden and spurt its potent load.

Then he stood and tugged at his short beard. "Yes. Remove their hair. But not with the sugar paste. You will shave them, allow them to feel and fear the blade. But you will make it the most sensual—" He laughed, a fiendish sound that began deep in his barrel chest "—and the last sexually arousing thing one of them will ever experience."

Mernoosh bit into a juicy date, then looked up at her husband. "What will happen to the other two?"

"They will die, too. In much the same way as the others."

"When?" Leila asked, alarmed that she might not have time to accomplish her goals.

"When I receive my orders to abandon this outpost and rejoin the main Republican Guard troop in Baghdad. As long as I must guard the oilfield, Lieutenant al Hassan and the American must be kept alive and healthy enough to supervise necessary repairs to the wells. The so-called engineer the colonel sent from Baghdad is an incompetent, but I dare not insist upon a replacement from the army now, with the Americans snapping at our borders."

"Will you take away their manhood first?"

Dubaq laid his sticky fingers on the exposed part of Leila's cheek. "Not if you choose to avail yourself of it, little scarred one. Is that your wish?"

"No—"

"Do not lie. You're as hot-blooded as Mernoosh. Yes. I know. Saqr was quite the braggart." Shrugging, he pulled his hand back and shook his head. "I would take you to my couch and ease your lust, but your scars repel me," he added, cupping the bulge in his uniform pants as though taunting Leila with what he would not share with her.

Not that she would welcome his carnal attention.

"If you wish, you may enjoy al Hassan for as long as he is whole. I will have him bound in such a way that you may ride him to pleasure, if that's your desire. And I will provide you a key in case you wish to free parts of him to pleasure you."

Leila smiled and nodded.

Perfect.

She might never again experience love, but she would feel the willing touch of a lover.

Even if it took the imminent threat of castration and death to make him willing.

* * * * *

Asad still breathed, though Jamil doubted his countryman was long for the world. He lay, naked, blood still dripping from the charred stub of his thumb that Dubaq had crudely amputated yesterday afternoon. The American, Brian Shearer, had recovered sufficiently from his own brutal beating to stand by his cot on shaky legs at the barked command from a fat, greasy guard.

"Remove your clothing, " one of the regular day guards ordered when he noticed Jamil had dressed.

Then he busied himself removing bloody blankets from Asad's unconscious body while Jamil watched, sickened that Dubaq would order further torture for a man obviously so near to the death he apparently had sought.

"Now!" the guard barked, louder this time.

Startled, Jamil lifted off the *dishdasha* he'd put on earlier and let it drop to his feet.

"What the fuck?" The American's mouth had dropped open, his expression making the awful bruises on his pallid skin almost unremarkable.

Jamil followed Shearer's gaze to his crotch. "A ball stretcher. Courtesy of those who guard us," he said in English, hoping this guard would not understand.

"Remove that, too, al Hassan," the other guard said, gesturing toward the leather as he roughly spread Jamil's legs and clamped his ankles into leg irons that had been chained to iron eyelets embedded in the wall.

Jamil struggled to maintain his balance while he unbuckled the ball stretcher and handed it to the guard. A grin on his ugly face, the guard grabbed one arm at a time, shackling them to the wall at ninety-degree angles from Jamil's body.

Used to the procedure, except that this time he was shackled with his back instead of his face to the wall, Jamil bent his head from force of habit when the guard moved to position a heavy iron collar and clamp it tightly around his neck.

Another guard had shackled the American in a similar pose by the time Dubaq strode into the bunker pushing a battered stainless steel cart. Jamil squelched an oath when he guessed the probable purpose of the wicked-looking tools laid out on its surface.

Straight razors. Scalpels of various sizes and shapes. Needles and suturing materials. A brazier filled with glowing coals and a selection of bandages.

"Your grooming has been sadly neglected," the jailer said, picking up a razor while focusing his beady gaze first on the American, then on Jamil. "That will be remedied. I'd not want any of you to die of infection before learning what it feels like to be a eunuch. Leila, you may begin by shaving the unconscious one," he concluded when a heavily veiled woman joined him by the cart.

Jamil's balls tightened when the woman lifted another one of the razors. It was as though they sensed danger, the way they drew up toward his body. A chill spread from the iron shackles that bound his ankles, wrists, and neck through skin and flesh sensitized by exposure and daily beatings.

Razor in hand, Dubaq approached Jamil. "Do you not beg, Kuwaiti dog?" he jeered, taking a swipe down Jamil's body with the naked blade, stopping when he reached the base of his flaccid cock. "Perhaps I shall cut off your *lingam* as well as your seed sac. Yes, I believe I will."

Laughing, Dubaq grasped Jamil's genitals in one beefy hand and tugged them, hard. Though tears stung Jamil's cheeks, he refused to grant the jailer the satisfaction of hearing him cry out at the excruciating pain.

Blood dripped from yesterday's wounds that the razor swipe had reopened. Jamil swallowed reflexively and felt the bite of the collar on his throat. He spat at Dubaq. "I will never beg, Iraqi pervert."

Dubaq's fist came up hard and drew blood from a cut on Jamil's cheek. "Were you not chained as you are for a purpose, I would adjust your position and use your Kuwaiti ass to ease my lust. Or your mouth. But you will be more docile once relieved of your balls. Perhaps then I will no longer need to chain you in order to have you serve my pleasure."

"Come quickly, Dubaq. I believe this man is dead."

Jamil turned his head, followed the jailer's path to Asad's bed where the woman stood, the razor in her hand still dripping with shaving foam. Seeing him lying still and pale as death, Jamil realized Asad could not survive more torture. *Insha'Allah*, his countryman would soon find paradise.

It was as though something had broken in Asad's mind these past weeks, from the way he had abandoned his docile manner and begun taunting his captors far beyond the insults Jamil had spat out in futile defiance since the day of their capture. Asad had seemingly invited them to accelerate their torture.

They had. Dubaq had kept Asad chained to the wall by his cot for days at a time, subjecting him to hourly beatings while allowing him only occasional sips of water to assuage his thirst. Then, ten days ago, he'd begun hacking off Asad's fingers one by one.

The jailer stood over Asad's body, letting out a stream of vicious Arabic curses.

"Do you wish to take his manhood now?" the woman asked.

"Stupid woman. I'd not unman a corpse." Dubaq yelled for one of the guards. "Dispose of the body," he said, eyeing Asad's earthly remains in apparent disgust.

The woman glanced first at the American, then at Jamil. "Who would you have me prepare first?"

"Al Hassan." Dubaq shot a chilling look Jamil's way.

The woman came to him, her movement flowing beneath an ankle-length tunic that skimmed her slender curves. A purple silk *hijab* hid her face and neck except for dark eyes that Jamil found hauntingly familiar.

Kneeling between his legs as she was, she was out of his range of vision while she brushed foam over his calves and thighs and scraped it off with her blade. But he felt her calloused fingers when she stroked his newly denuded skin and the damp warmth of a cloth she used to cleanse the areas where he'd been shaved.

She had gentle fingers. Too soft a touch for a woman who was calmly preparing him to lose his balls.

Apparently Dubaq had chosen to refine his torture by letting this woman graphically remind Jamil of the capacity for carnal pleasure that he was about to lose forever.

He braced himself for the tug of the blade on the sensitive skin around his genitals, but it didn't come.

Instead, she stood and began using scissors to clip his hair and the scruffy beard he hadn't been allowed to shave or trim for months. Lather followed, and then the blade.

His head and neck. His arms, chest, and belly. Each in their turn, they were lathered, shaved, and wiped clean with a hot, wet towel.

No woman had cleansed his body for eleven long years. Rarely allowed to bathe himself during his enslavement, he reveled in the sensation of warmth, smoothness—the cleanliness he'd dreamed of many times as he lay shackled on his cot, wishing he could scratch away caked-on grime that made him itch and filled his nostrils with the stench of his own unwashed flesh.

His cock rose, as if defying the jailer.

"Eager, are you?" she murmured in Arabic, taking him in her hand and rubbing the pad of her thumb over his cock head. "Your slit weeps. Could it be you would like to put this juicy plum inside my *yoni*?"

"No."

She held his cock first to one side and then the other, using the scissors first before taking the razor up again to rid him of his pubic hair. "Liar. Your *lingam* says you would."

Trussed to the wall as he was for all to see, Jamil could hardly deny his obvious arousal. With each stroke of the woman's blade against his crotch, he wondered if the slash from Dubaq's knife would immediately follow her ministrations. He heard but could not see the jailer taunting the American prisoner while someone—another woman from the sound of her—apparently prepared him similarly to become a eunuch.

Desperate now, Jamil realized that if he didn't escape soon he would die painfully here in this hell, the same as Asad had just done. He had no choice but to approach Maktoum.

Then he must free himself and the American from their chains. Overpower their guards, perhaps steal a truck, and drive nearly seventy kilometers to safety in Kuwait, over roads so close to the borders that they were certain to be heavily patrolled.

Not likely. The Iraqi jailers' chains held fast. Jamil had tested them often enough over the years of his captivity.

But he would have to try. And while he thought it possible that Maktoum would take a message to Dahoud, he had no illusion that the guard would risk his own painful death by releasing prisoners from their chains.

The warm, wet cloth soothed Jamil's freshly shaven cock and balls. Aroused him further despite his fear that Dubaq would now sever them as he'd threatened to do so often for the past eleven years. Then he felt cool air and warm, damp breath bathing his sensitized flesh.

"Would you feel my *yoni* or Dubaq's knife?" the woman asked quietly.

"Are you telling me I have a choice?"

She stood and looked him in the eye. With his legs spread as they were, they were of an equal height. "For a time. Until you give me the child your people and the Americans denied me. Then Dubaq will assure himself that my child will be the last to spring from your loins."

Suddenly Jamil knew. This was Dubaq's scarred sister-by-marriage. She wore *hijab* not to hide her attributes as much as to conceal the burn scars he'd noticed when she had brought him food and water while he worked in the oilfield. The guards had talked about her, mentioning how she'd acquired the scars during the Americans' bombings of Baghdad.

"Why me, Leila? Why do you wish your enemy to father your son?"

"Who else, here in this desolate place? You are an attractive man. I want a child, but I'd not subject myself to groping by one of the loutish men who answer to Dubaq."

"And I could not grope you because I was in chains?" Suddenly his phantom lover of the night before took on a voice. A face. A substance unlike the shadowy apparition who had taken him in the dark of night.

He had not dreamed. Leila had come to him last night, ridden his cock to pleasure—hers and his own.

She is as sexually deprived as I.

She moved so close that he felt her heat. "I could have your bonds loosened so that you might pleasure me with your hands."

And if you do, I will find a way to escape this living hell.

Part of Jamil recoiled at the thought of seducing one of Dubaq's kin, even if the relationship was only by marriage. But then he remembered Asad's screams. The physical torture he and the others had endured at their jailers' hands. Torture and mutilation that had killed them one by one until only he remained.

Jamil had avoided the worst of the torture until now, except for having endured the humiliation and pain of repeated rapes by Dubaq and his men. The ball stretcher he'd worn since the first time Dubaq had invaded his ass while others took turns fucking his mouth served as a constant reminder that his balls, if not his very life, lay in the jailer's evil hands.

Yes, he'd fuck the devil himself if it meant he might gain a chance, however faint, for escape. And Leila was not the devil. Jamil thrust his hips forward, ignoring the bite of his shackles. His cock lodged itself between Leila's slightly spread thighs.

"I have been starved for years, *houri*. Starved for the sweet honey of a hot, wet pussy. I want to feast on yours while you suck my cock and balls," he whispered. "For me to do that, my shackles must be removed."

"Perhaps I will loosen your bonds if you please me."

Her lips curved in a smile, and she closed her thighs around his cock. "Now I must go. I will come to your cell after dark."

When she did, Jamil would seek to accommodate her so fully she would want more. She would want the sexual pleasures he could provide only if she removed his bonds—and those of his fellow prisoner.

Entrapped

Chapter Three

ಸಾ

"I thought my balls were goners."

The American, Air Force Lieutenant Brian Shearer, could not have realized until arriving here how lucky he'd been to have served his years of enslavement elsewhere. "Unless we find a means of escape, they soon will be," Jamal said. "Dubaq, our jailer, enjoys inflicting all forms of torture—mental as well as physical."

He looked around for the guard who had chained him and Shearer loosely to the malfunctioning pumpjack they'd been brought out here to repair. There he was. As always, the man had found a shady spot beneath a cluster of date palms.

"Hold this wrench." Jamil bent over the rusty pump, pretending to make adjustments to it. "Tonight Dubaq's sister will come to me."

Quickly he laid out his plan to seduce her, gain her trust, propose a *ménage à trois* so she would remove the chains from Brian as well as Jamil, and overpower her and the guard who watched over them at night.

"I could not. I promised my wife—"

"Your wife would not ask you to choose faithfulness over life, would she?"

The American paused. "I don't think so."

"It will only be one time. To gain her trust. The next night we will make our escape."

Allah grant him patience! Of all the American soldiers who could have been sent to Dubaq's prison bunker, why must it have been one whose sense of moral righteousness might outweigh his need to survive?

"How far are we from the Kuwaiti border?" Shearer asked.

Relieved, Jamil let out his breath. The American would go along with his plan, no matter how distasteful he found the prospect of engaging in sex with a woman other than his wife. "Less than seventy kilometers, but the desert is not forgiving. *Insha'Allah*, I will be able to get word to members of my family to meet us at the border, near *Abdali*."

"Kuwaiti dog! Have you not yet completed the repairs on that pump?" their guard yelled from his spot at the trunk of a date palm tree.

"No. I must take the engine apart. That will take more sunlight than is left this day," Jamil said, sending a quelling look Shearer's way. "Quiet. As long as there is work for us to complete, we may have another day to live. Another day to remain men."

The guard ambled over to them, unhooked their chains from the pumpjack, and tugged them back to the bunker.

* * * * *

Night descended, casting the bunker in shadows. Dubaq himself oversaw the shackling of the American while he allowed Jamil the rare privilege of washing away the day's grime from his freshly shaved skin.

"Enjoy my wife's sister-by-marriage, Kuwaiti, for she will be the last woman you ever pleasure. Tomorrow you had best find a way to make that pump work. I have a quota of oil to produce from this field your countrymen nearly destroyed." The jailer grabbed Jamil's testicles, twisting the sac so viciously Jamil cried out from the pain. "If you do not, the American can pleasure Leila in your stead, because you will be dead."

Dubaq shoved Jamil onto his cot and secured his wrists and ankles with the heavy chains. "I will leave the collar off so you may move your head freely," he said, tossing the collar into the corner where it clanked ominously against the heavy chain to which it was attached. "I imagine she'll find good use for your Kuwaiti tongue."

* * * * *

Leila splayed her fingers over her breasts and belly, savoring the tactile sensations while she bathed. As always, the lack of feeling on the areas of her body that had been burned reminded her of her ugliness. Of hideous memories she could not escape.

Perhaps the Kuwaiti would not mind. After all, he bore scars, too. But not like hers.

No. Like a creature of the night, she must come to him in darkness. Keep him bound so he would not feel her shame.

She must take. Never share the pleasure as she once had done with Saqr.

Leila rose and let the warm dry air caress her willingly, as she believed no man would do again. A crescent moon hung in the night sky, lending its faint light through a window.

A night for lovers?

He was hardly her lover. Not when his choices were fucking her or facing the kind of gruesome death Dubaq enjoyed meting out. She'd not delude herself.

After massaging fruity oil into her freshly denuded arms, legs, and *yoni*, Leila draped a thin silk chemise over her body. Her nipples tightened against the gold rings that pierced them. Slick, arousing sensation coursed through her veins when she dragged her fingers against the aching nubs. How much better the Kuwaiti's velvety tongue and sculpted lips would feel when he licked and suckled her there.

But that would not happen. Leila would content herself with devouring his beautiful *lingam*, fondling the velvety seed sac that Dubaq would soon cut from his body. While she sucked his juicy plum and fondled his doomed testicles, perhaps she would order him to pleasure her *yoni* with his tongue, the way Saqr used to do.

Yes, she would force the prisoner to pleasure her first with his mouth. Then she would mount him and ride him to paradise.

As she'd done so many times for her husband's pleasure, she lifted her chemise and threaded a thin gold chain through her nipple rings and the small hoop that pierced her navel. Though the Kuwaiti would never see her adornments, feeling the slight weight of the chain would titillate her own senses.

By the time she'd veiled herself and made her way across the sand to the prison bunker, Leila's *yoni* was dripping with anticipation.

Tonight the light in the bunker was brighter. Jamil was lying as Dubaq had said he would be, chained to his cot. His position was the same as it had been the night before, except that now he did not have the iron collar clamped about his neck.

Her mouth watered at the sight of his satiny golden skin, his muscular torso, and the massive organ that for the coming days was hers to enjoy. Already half-hard as though anticipating her arrival, his *lingam* invited her to taste him, learn whether it was as hot and silky as it looked rising up from his freshly denuded scrotal sac.

Allah! He was magnificent.

When he met her gaze, he smiled as though he looked forward to having her use his *lingam* for her pleasure. When she felt her facial muscles contract, she realized that despite herself she had smiled back at him.

Her fingers knotted in the fabric of her tunic, and she began to lift it off.

No. She could not bear to watch his gaze turn cold, his handsome face contort into a mask of disgust. Leila let the tunic drop to the floor again as she approached her helpless love slave.

"Please. I would look upon you, *houri*."

He sounded so sincere, she almost believed him. Almost. "Silence. This is about my pleasure, not yours."

Sitting on the edge of the cot, her outer thigh pressed against his side, she uncapped a vial of fragrant oil laced with the fruit enzymes that would inhibit the regrowth of hair on the prisoner's magnificent body.

The heady scent of apricots, spiced with cinnamon and cloves and cardamon, filled her nostrils when she poured some of the oil onto her hands. Her fingers tingled at their initial contact with the smooth, supple skin that stretched over Jamil's hard-muscled chest.

Those muscles rippled when she slid her oiled hands over them, around small coppery nipples that puckered against her fingertips. Sleek, like heavy satin and warm, sweet cream, his skin absorbed the oil, taking on a golden glow in the light from harsh incandescent fixtures.

When she moved lower, his *lingam* came to full attention. Like the petals of a lotus on the riverbank, it unfurled, stretching and hardening as it rose over his belly. He moaned, then strained against his wrist restraints as though he wanted to touch her, too.

A shudder wracked his body when she rubbed her thumb over the ruby head of his penis. As if mourning its enslavement, its single eye wept a milky tear.

An iridescent liquid pearl centered on the bulging ruby head of his erection.

She had to taste it. Taste him. And she wanted him to drink her honey, too.

Dubaq had given her so little time to fulfill her long-denied needs with the Kuwaiti prisoner.

Leila cupped his scrotum, unable to prevent the tears that came when she remembered this beautiful part of him would soon be gone. Tenderly she massaged in the oil there and around his puckered anus, before moving on to massage the satiny skin of his muscular thighs and calves.

If she freed him from his chains she could oil his back, as well.

Dubaq had entrusted her with the key that would unlock his shackles.

But no. She dared not.

Her *yoni* dripped, and her abdominal muscles clenched when she bent to taste her prisoner's glistening *lingam*. Unable to wait longer, she lifted her tunic and straddled his handsome face. "Pleasure me," she ordered, lowering herself until his hot, damp breath seared her most sensitive flesh.

His tongue snaked out, sought, and found her swollen sex.

"More." She slid lower, felt his mouth opening, sucking her inside.

His teeth grazed her clitoris, then caught it for his tongue to flail.

When she arched her back, the chain that connected her piercings tightened. It tugged at her nipples the way she wished she dared order him to do.

Perhaps soon, if she could make him as hot for her as she was for him…

She is my enemy. And she is raping me now as surely as I was raped when Dubaq chained me to the wall and used me like a whore. Humiliating me in plain sight of the guard and within the hearing of the American.

But when Jamil inhaled her musk, the scent of fruit and spices in the oil she'd obviously used on her pussy as well as on him, he smelled woman.

A hot, desirable woman. A woman he intended to use to achieve his freedom.

His tongue tingled at the tart, heady taste of her when she arched her back, settling her clit more firmly between his open lips.

As his eyes grew accustomed to the darkness created by her tunic that had settled over his face and chest, he was able to make out her anus, the gently rounded shape of her buttocks and the tops of firm, silky thighs.

Thighs he felt against his cheeks and ached to touch. When the shackles bit into the flesh of his wrists, he realized he'd reached out for her in truth as well as in his mind.

Surely it would hurt no one if he allowed himself to enjoy the seduction, whatever its purpose.

He opened his mouth wider, stabbed his tongue into her dripping pussy. The loosely woven fabric of her tunic scraped his slick, oiled torso when she bent over and lowered her mouth to his sex. Not wanting to end his feast, he lifted his head and sucked in the moist, soft flesh around her swollen clit.

His cock swelled to nearly bursting when he felt her warm breath. The wet, warm slide of her lips and the gentle scrape of her teeth over its sensitive slit, its swollen head. Its throbbing length. And by the time he felt her throat convulsing around his cock head, her hot damp breath was bathing his balls in delicious sensation.

She tasted sweet tonight. Too sweet to resist. Starved too long for a woman's softness, Jamil drank his fill and reveled in the sensual torture of feeling her swallowing his cock, bathing his clean, smoothly shaven scrotum with heat and moisture while she cradled his balls in her hands.

Sensations bombarded him, made him crazy. Trying to ignore the cruel bite of his leg shackles, he dug his ass into the cot, then arched his back to increase the friction from her lips as she took him down her throat again.

Leila swallowed harder, ran her tongue up and down a prominent vein in his *lingam* that throbbed in an accelerating rhythm. Delicious sensations flowed to her *yoni* from his velvety tongue, his teeth. From the pressure of his soft lips clamped firmly over her labia and holding her open for his sensual assault.

Pressure built inside her, threatened to overflow. She sucked him harder and felt rather than heard his moan that reverberated off her swollen flesh.

He couldn't come now. Not yet. She slid his penis out of her mouth and began to lick his satiny scrotum.

The rasping sound of the guard's labored breathing bounced off the concrete walls. Was the odious man's *lingam* hard, and did his heart beat faster? Was he using his hand to do what he was watching her do to his helpless prisoner with her mouth?

Was the American straining at his bonds in the adjacent cell as he listened to the anguished moans and the slapping, sucking sounds of sexual feasting? Was his *lingam* swollen nearly to the bursting point while he lay chained, unable to reach his own sex and see to his release?

Imagining the American writhing on his cot in an agony of sexual deprivation gave Leila a sense of poetic justice. After all, it had been his countrymen who had made her a widow before her sixteenth birthday. His fellow pilots who had stolen her beauty with their bombs.

And knowing the guard could see her sucking the Kuwaiti's beautiful, doomed balls into her mouth one at a time while he lapped her honeyed *yoni* added an element of excitement that heightened Leila's pleasure.

Her vaginal muscles clenched around his seeking tongue.

When he grew even harder and she felt his *lingam* ooze a drop of slippery fluid against her cheek, she lifted her head. He was too close.

Inside. She wanted him to come inside her.

Slowly, for she meant to savor each sensation and every second of the prisoner's ravishment, she straightened. Reversed her position. Impaled herself inch by thick, pulsing inch on his throbbing organ.

He strained at his bonds, lifted his hips as if to deepen the penetration.

With a mighty heave and a shudder, he pushed into her. Stretched her. Loving the feeling, she lowered herself until his balls nestled within her inner labia.

"Free me, *houri,* and I will give you even greater pleasure. Certainly you cannot believe I could deny you now."

His whispered words penetrated her sexual haze, tempted her to release his shackles. She reached for the key Dubaq had given her.

Chapter Four

Small fingers gripped his wrist. Metal clinked on metal, and the jaws of the second handcuff sprang open.

But her pussy's iron grip on his cock stayed firm. She rode him like one of the ancient Tartars depicted in classic art. Back straight, she braced her hands on his chest in much the way a warrior might rest his hands upon his mount's sturdy neck.

Up and down. She gloved him in her moist, warm pussy, her inner muscles gripping and releasing him like tiny fists.

His leg irons held him open for her pleasure. Helpless to his own desire.

A large part of Jamil wanted to overpower her, unlock the shackles that still bit at his ankles and make a run for freedom. But now was not the time. He must treat his assailant as a lover, gain her trust, seduce her senses while she used his body as her carnal tool.

His throbbing cock demanded release. Release that was very close to bubbling from his loins.

Too close if he was to trap her in her own seductive game. Jamil breathed deeply, struggling to regain control.

His muscles aching from having been stretched for too long in the same uncomfortable position, he stroked along the outer curves of breasts cloaked in the thin fabric of her tunic.

Her little moan and the shudder that reverberated through his fingers made him bolder. With his thumbs, he found and circled her distended nipples.

And felt the jewelry she wore where none could see.

Somehow it made her seem more human. Less the scarred sister who lurked in the shadow of Dubaq's pregnant wife. And less the dominatrix taking her fill of his helpless body under the cover of night and garments that covered her from head to toe.

Before war had torn her world apart, had she loved and laughed and worn bright clothes? Had she danced naked for a lover the way Jamil had once expected his wife would someday dance for him, before that same war had snatched away his hopes and dreams?

He felt the chain and gave it a gentle tug. Her pussy clenched tighter around his cock, and her nipples tightened more against the pads of his thumbs.

"I wish to taste you here," he said as he pulled at both nipples and the chain that joined them. Then he lowered his hands, grasped the hem of her tunic.

"No." She flattened her body against his chest and grasped his seeking arms.

Her silk *hijab* tickled his cheek when he rubbed it against the side of her head. "Your scars will not repulse me."

"You cannot know this." As if to distract him, Leila moved faster, took his cock deeper with every downward stroke of her hips.

Jamil abandoned his quest to bare her breasts and sank his fingers into the firm, bare flesh of her bottom. When she attempted to free herself, he held her fast. "You are soft here," he said. "Much softer than the shroud you wear."

Warm, damp bursts tickled his neck, letting him know his touch aroused her, too. He felt rather than heard her tiny moan when he loosened his hold and began to stroke her trembling ass and thighs.

He loved how she seemed to respond to his slightest touch. The contractions of her pussy around his cock and the fresh gush of moisture onto his balls told more than the harder, faster, almost desperate pace of her fucking.

She was about to come.

And so was he. Clasping her silk-shrouded head in his hands, he dragged her down until their mouths met. Fucked her mouth with his tongue the way she was fucking herself on his cock. He encircled her slender body with his arms when her pussy spasmed around him, and he shot burst after burst of semen into her demanding womb.

"I would be the one to ride you, *houri*. Would you release me from my chains?" he whispered later as she lay on him, her energy spent.

"Perhaps tomorrow, my prisoner."

* * * * *

Her prisoner. No longer could she think of Jamil as her slave. Pleasantly sated from last night's sexual feast, Leila sipped her strong, sweet coffee and picked a plump date from the plate in the center of the table.

"We must prepare to return to Baghdad. I received word the Americans are expected to attack any day," Dubaq told Mernoosh. "My men will be needed to fight."

"When?" Mernoosh asked.

"In three days' time. First the Kuwaiti must complete the repairs I have been ordered to see done in the oilfield."

Leila's mouth went dry, and her pulse quickened. "Will we take the prisoners when we go?"

"Foolish woman. They will die here. Do you think I want witnesses if I am dragged before the courts our enemies promise for those who they will claim have committed crimes against humanity?"

Dubaq's beady eyes glittered when he spoke of murder. And Mernoosh seemed not to care what atrocities her husband might have committed. Might still commit.

But Leila wanted the Kuwaiti to live. "I have not yet had my fill of the Kuwaiti," she said before she could hold back the words.

"Let him pleasure her while he lives, husband. It is not as though some worthy man might choose to take her to his couch." Mernoosh stroked Dubaq's thigh, as if to remind Leila she had a man while Leila did not.

Dubaq laughed. "It shall be as you say. I have no time to make his and the American's deaths slow and memorable. Perhaps the American..." He paused, as though considering the degree of pain he might inflict in three short days. "No. If we are to close this camp, I have no time to devote to torture. They shall die together before we take our leave."

So soon? As Leila went about the chore of packing her sister's meager household effects that morning, she realized she had but three short days to take her fill of Jamil. Three nights to lie in his embrace and take her pleasure.

She wanted more.

And she didn't want Jamil to die for no better reason than to save Dubaq the risk of having witnesses to testify in some future court trial as to the extent of his brutality.

She reminded herself Jamil was an enemy.

Yes, Jamil had probably killed Iraqis. So had the American. More to the point, their allies had killed Saqr. But those killings had been the byproducts of waging war. Dubaq, she realized, relished killing for killing's sake.

He certainly took pleasure in torture. She'd cringed at the evidence of brutal beatings, seeing prisoners paraded about with newly severed fingers and toes. And hearing anguished screams from the bunker during amputations and castrations performed by her brother-in-law's own hands. Dubaq had obviously relished each and every act of brutality that had preceded the deaths of his prisoners.

Leila recounted thirteen brutal murders since she and Mernoosh had arrived at the encampment. Allah only knew how many there might have been in the years before that.

Blood pounded in her head. Her fingers tingled not at the memory of how Jamil's muscles had rippled beneath them last night, but at the thought of the previous day and how that other prisoner's cool, clammy flesh had grown colder each moment while she'd wielded a razor, preparing him for his final humiliation before death.

At least the man named Asad had cheated Dubaq of his last fiendish act of pleasure. He had entered paradise still a man.

Leila should not care. The Kuwaiti she was using meant nothing to her. Nothing but a *lingam*, hands, and a mouth to bring her pleasure. That they were attached to a human with a heart and soul and feelings should make no difference.

But even now she might be carrying Jamil's child. What would that child think if he learned one day that his mother had raped his father and then allowed him to be unceremoniously slaughtered like a lamb for a feast?

Folding Mernoosh's best hand-woven table covering and placing it in a box for transport, Leila tried to put Jamil from her mind. There was nothing she could do to change his fate even if she tried. But she could not help remembering how good it felt when she released the chains from his wrists and he held her in his arms.

In her own way, Leila cared for the first man who had brought her pleasure since Saqr's untimely death. What if anything she could do to save him, however, remained a mystery.

* * * * *

As soon as the two other guards were out of hearing range, Jamil made his proposition to Maktoum, the Marsh Arab who usually guarded him but who had been ordered to work with him and Brian today on the damaged pump. A proposition that could easily backfire and end Jamil's life before the sun went down.

"What makes you think I would betray my countrymen?" Maktoum asked after Jamil spelled out his request.

Jamil chose his words carefully. "Your countrymen have betrayed your people, left you to become their minions or starve. You appear to cringe at the atrocities Dubaq has committed on his helpless prisoners." Pausing, he looked the Marsh Arab in the eye. "And once you get to Kuwait, my cousin will pay you well."

Maktoum's black eyes glittered, and his thin lips curved up in semblance of a smile. "What is in it for me besides money? I could earn a few *dinars* more safely by continuing my work for the army."

"Freedom. And it's not a few *dinars* you will earn, but more than you've ever seen. My family is wealthy and loves me well."

"You wish me to go tonight?" the man asked as though he'd made his decision.

Jamil no longer had the luxury of time. Not with Dubaq's men scurrying about, packing equipment and ammunition while they talked about returning to Baghdad in preparation for an American invasion.

His days were numbered. Besides, tonight was not one of Maktoum's nights to guard the prison bunker. If he didn't set his plans in motion now, he might never have another opportunity. "Yes. It must be tonight. "

Jamil explained how Maktoum must cross the border into Kuwait, contact his cousin Dahoud el Rashid, and enlist his help with the planned escape. "Can you remember all this?"

"Yes. But if I am to do it, you must do something for me. Not *dinars*, though they will be most appreciated. You must bring with you my grandfather, Zayed. He cannot survive here alone. And you must know I cannot return."

Jamil had no doubt the vengeance Dubaq would take on one of his own who had betrayed him would involve a slow and painful death. Although he did not quite believe the guard's assurances that his elderly grandfather could hold his own on the arduous journey they faced, he agreed to take him with them.

It was clearly a condition Maktoum would not negotiate.

And it was equally obvious to Jamil that it was in his own best interests not to complete the repairs on the pump today.

If he and the American were still here when the pump repair was finished or when Dubaq pulled his troop out of this prison camp, whichever came first, Dubaq was going to kill them. Logic told Jamil their deaths, if it came to that, would be quicker and less painful if delayed until the moment of the troop's departure.

Insha'Allah, before that time came Maktoum would have reached Dahoud and help would be on the way. He and the American would have escaped alive from the hellish bunker that had been his home for eleven years. And the guard's elderly grandfather would have been found to possess the strength and endurance of a camel. He would require such traits to endure the arduous trek across the desert.

As he fiddled with the mechanism that controlled the flow of oil into the main pipeline under the watchful eye of one of Dubaq's men, Jamil mentally plotted his desperate attempt to hold onto life—and regain his freedom in the bargain.

* * * * *

I don't want to do this, Diane.

In spite of himself, Brian lay chained to his cot, his cock as hard as stone as he listened to the sounds of Jamil having sex with the Iraqi woman as they bounced off the concrete bunker walls. Slapping sounds and low-pitched moans reminded him of the bride he hadn't seen for eleven long years. The hot, sweet nights they'd shared before he had shipped out to fly his F-15 in the Gulf War.

"Two of us can give you twice the pleasure, *houri*," Jamil said, his words punctuated by the woman's orgasmic scream. "Imagine my cock in your pussy like this, and his in your mouth. Or your sweet, tight ass."

"Do you truly want to share this with another man?"

"I want but to satisfy you. If it takes more than one of us..."

"It does not. More. Ohhh." She sounded the way Diane used to, just before she came. "Do not stop."

"His cock would fill you better than my fingers."

Apparently Jamil was having no better luck persuading the woman to release them both than Brian was having, fighting the futile urge to rip loose his chains and take care of his raging hard-on with his hand.

And the conversation Brian heard clearly through the thin wall that connected his and the Kuwaiti's cells made his balls tighten, his dick harden and throb against his belly. Involuntarily, his hips lifted as though there were a hot, wet woman just out of reach.

Hard breathing. Moans. Simultaneous screams of satisfaction told Brian his fellow prisoner and the Iraqi woman had achieved what he was denied.

Then silence, as though they rested for the next bout of erotic sport.

"He can hear us, you know," Jamil said while Brian lay in an agony of unfulfilled lust, unable to relieve himself. "Do you not want to let the American join in our pleasure?"

"I am no whore, Kuwaiti. Besides, you satisfy me well. I need no other man."

More than the woman's hormones were tied up with Jamil. She would, Brian imagined, set Jamil free before she would watch their jailer kill him. Perhaps she would let him go, too, if his fellow prisoner asked her to.

Brian willed his erection to subside, half relieved that she had rejected Jamil's suggestion of a *ménage à trois*. If he managed to survive and escape this hell, Brian would have the satisfaction of knowing he'd remained faithful to Diane.

Chapter Four

೩೦

Under the desert moon, Maktoum pulled the ancient GAZ personnel carrier he had stolen off the road, abandoned it, and crept silently toward the Kuwaiti border three kilometers away, keeping well away from the rutted roadway.

Sweat rolled off his brow, caused more by icy terror than by the heat of the night. He had no illusions about what would happen to him if he were caught in this no-man's land. He would be a dead man.

Dubaq, the monster captain of the oilfield and prison regiment Maktoum had just deserted, would undoubtedly see to it that his death would be slow and painful. Death here at the hands of the border guards would at least be quick and relatively merciful.

The note Maktoum carried from the Kuwaiti prisoner weighed heavily in the pocket of the dingy brown robe he wore over worn-out army fatigues. Its color, he hoped, would blend with the desert sand and keep him from attracting the attention of guards he knew would be stationed at the checkpoint on the border.

A falcon swooped down from the sky and caught an unsuspecting desert snake, reminding him that danger came not only from creatures on the ground but from above.

Close. He was close now. Sounds of men talking in Arabic rang in his ears. Not the Arabic he had been taught, but some incomprehensible dialect. Had he crossed into Kuwait already?

He did not know. But he was certain the Kuwaiti town of *Abdali* lay on the road he had recently abandoned, not far beyond the border with Iraq. It was there where the prisoner had said he could find a telephone and contact this Dahoud el Rashid who would fill his pockets with Kuwaiti *dinars*.

The journey had been difficult, even though he had covered most of the distance in the stolen truck. His legs ached, and he gasped to force air beyond the constriction in his chest.

Maktoum tried not to think of how much more difficult his grandfather Zayed's trip would be, made on foot in the company of the two condemned prisoners.

But the old man had yearned to die free. And this was most likely his last chance to escape the tyranny he hated so much.

Nearly ninety years old, Zayed had outlived three wars, four wives, ten sons and daughters, and all of his thirty-eight grandchildren except Maktoum. Perhaps he would survive to escape the oppression he had endured for years under Saddam Hussein's despotic rule.

There. Maktoum saw shadows in the darkness. He blinked, thinking it was an illusion. But they were still there. And there were lights. He must have crossed into Kuwait moments earlier, and that must be *Abdali* in the distance. Excited, he increased his pace, less wary now of being seen. Surely the letter from the prisoner would save him now, should he stumble into the hands of Kuwaiti soldiers.

Unless the soldiers should decide to kill him first and ask questions later.

When Maktoum reached an army outpost much larger than the one the prisoner had described, his mention of the name of the man he had been instructed to contact brought him not a jail cell but a phone and refreshments, both supplied with shocking speed.

He quenched his thirst with a cold, sweet fruit drink as he dialed the number Jamil had given him for Dahoud el Rashid.

* * * * *

"Hello." Shana el Rashid stretched out on the sleeping couch, her sleek naked body brushing her husband's when she reached over him to get the phone. "Bear, it's for you. I can't understand what the man wants."

Bear groaned. Damn it, he hated having his sleep interrupted for any reason other than to pleasure his beloved wife. "Another problem at the new oilfield, I suppose," he mumbled, taking the phone.

"Dahoud el Rashid here," he said in Arabic into the offending instrument. "What in Allah's name is so important that it can't wait until morning?"

But it wasn't the assistant foreman he had expected to hear. This was a man who called himself Maktoum. He spoke a strange dialect of Arabic and said what Bear thought meant he was delivering a message from his lost cousin, Jamil al Hassan.

Jamil? "Slow down, Maktoum. Tell me again that my cousin lives and that he wants my help."

Wide awake now, Bear snatched up a pad and pen, and scribbled down information as Maktoum blurted it out. Damn. He could hardly make out what the man was saying, other than to catch a few words and try to string them into something comprehensible. "You are in *Abdali*?"

Turning to Shana, he covered the mouthpiece. "Get me a map, love. And find a place called *Abdali*. It's in northern Kuwait, in *Al Jahrah* province near the Iraqi border."

A moment later she returned, kneeling beside him with the map spread out on the couch. With a long, painted fingernail, she pointed out a small town about halfway between *Al Jahrah* and *Al Basrah*, just across the border from Iraq.

"I see where it is now. We will meet you there," he said into the phone before hanging up and pulling Shana into his arms.

"Jamil lives," he told her, his hands unsteady as he digested the unexpected news. Holding out a hand, he steadied Shana when she rose gracefully off the carpet by the couch. "*Insha'Allah*, he will succeed in this scheme to escape his captors."

A smile lit her beautiful face. She'd said all along that they would have sensed it if Bear's young cousin had died when his plane had gone down during the Gulf War. "I told you he'd come back. Who was that?"

"A prison guard, apparently a Marsh Arab from his dialect. I couldn't understand a lot of what he said, but I gather he felt his interests would be best served by assisting Jamil in his escape. I leave for *Abdali* at first light."

"Surely you won't go alone."

When her arms tightened about his waist, his cock came to life against the softness of her slender belly. "I will take Jake if he can pry himself away from his bride, and two of the oilfield workers."

"You must bring Jamil here."

"I will." Where else did his cousin have to go since the Iraqi invaders had destroyed his home near Al Wafrah and killed his parents? "He may have others with him," Bear told Shana, recalling a few snippets of Maktoum's message that he thought he'd understood correctly.

"The more the merrier. They will all be welcome."

"Good. Should the Iraqi dogs attempt crossing into Kuwait to recapture them, they will be safer here than they would be, closer to the border."

A shudder went through Shana's slender body. "Tell me more about this rescue you're planning."

"Jake and I, and two of my oilfield workers who know how to handle weapons will fly to *Abdali* in the morning. We will meet with this Maktoum and learn exactly where we are to pick up Jamil and his companions."

It was fortuitous that Shana's brother had decided to spend part of his honeymoon here at their villa. Having another qualified helicopter pilot onboard might mean the difference between success and failure since Bear's regular chopper pilot was away on holiday.

Shana pulled away and looked him in the eye. "Tell me you aren't going into Iraq. Bear, this is a job for the Army."

"I won't know until we get to *Abdali*. But trust me, love, I have no desire to risk my neck. Or to lose the life we have made together here for ourselves and our family. There will be no shortage of soldiers near the border. The American army is conducting exercises with Kuwaiti troops along the northern border with Iraq."

Deliberately, he stroked her back, stoking the sexual fire that always smoldered just below the surface in his wife, even now after eleven years of marriage. "Come back to bed. Warm me."

When she lay back down, he didn't join her but knelt at the edge of the couch and parted her silky legs. Draping them over his shoulders as he caught her clit ring on the tip of his tongue, he played with it and ran his palms along the skin of her inner thighs.

"You're not going to distract me no matter how hard you try," she told him.

But the catch in her voice and her rapid breathing told him he was well on the way to banishing everything but sexual pleasure from Shana's mind. Accelerating his assault, Bear slid his hands up her body until he cupped both of her firm, full breasts.

Her nipples already jutted forward, hard little buttons pierced with gold barbells that secured the sapphire-encrusted nipple shields he'd found in an Egyptian bazaar. When he rubbed his thumbs over their tips, they hardened more, as though begging for the suction of his mouth and tongue.

But his tongue was busy elsewhere, flicking her swollen clit and toying with the tiny gold ring she'd had inserted there three months earlier during their visit with her ailing father in Houston.

She'd told him she'd had it put there for her own pleasure, but the tiny piece of jewelry had proven arousing to him as well.

His balls tightened when he tasted her wet, warm pussy and stroked the satiny skin that covered her breasts and belly. *Insha'Allah*, he would never lose Shana, the woman who'd held his heart since she'd asked him nearly twelve years ago to fulfill her fantasy of becoming a captive *houri* to an Arab sheikh.

"No fair. I want my fun, too. And I can't reach your cock when you're way down there."

Bear wiggled his tongue in her pussy for a minute before climbing up to join her on the couch. "Think you'd like it if I got one of those rings through my cock?" he asked, tugging gently on her clit ring as he knelt between her legs and rubbed his cock head along her hot, wet labia before sinking deep inside her tight, welcoming sheath.

Her talented inner muscles that clasped his cock seemed to get stronger instead of weaker as time passed.

"Mmmm. Maybe. Oh, God. Your cock feels so good inside me. I don't think you need to do anything to make it better. Oh, yesss. Like that, my sheikh. Harder." She let out the little moan of pleasure he loved to hear, then shook her head and laughed. "There must be something wrong with us, still fucking like minks every day after all these years."

Her next breathy scream told him he'd hit her G-spot, and that she liked it. A lot.

"Fate, love. Allah brought me my perfect *houri*, all the way from Houston. Come again with me," he coaxed, sinking deeper into her with every measured motion of his hips.

Her breathing grew shallow. Sweat glistened on her brow. They moved together in perfect harmony, two lovers for whom time had heightened sensations and brought them as close to being one entity as a man and a woman could become.

Her vaginal muscles clenched his cock like a fist, pulsating and full of life. And when she dragged her nails down his back and clasped her legs around his waist like a vise, Bear let go of his iron control, shooting his load in hard, as she milked him dry with every undulating contraction of her pussy.

"Just think. Jamil has done without this for eleven long years," Shana murmured moments later. "I imagine he'll be ready to take on a couple of bimbos like the ones you hired that time—"

"Quiet, woman. Morning will come far too soon."

* * * * *

Sated from a night of hot but monogamous sex, Jamil wakened in his cot the following morning, his body unshackled but for Leila's slender arms and legs that twined about his naked body.

When he opened his eyes, he noticed her scarf and veil had slipped during the night, exposing short, silky black hair and the creamy skin of her cheek and neck that had remained untouched by the fierce desert sun. Idly, he stroked her there, regretting that when he lay with her tonight he would betray her trust—the trust she had exhibited when she had not confined him again once she had achieved her sexual satisfaction.

Her eyelids fluttered, and she leaned into his body momentarily before jerking away and adjusting the scarf about her head and neck.

"Your scars are marks of valor, Leila. They do not repel me."

"Do not lie, Kuwaiti."

"My name is Jamil." He pressed his swollen cock against her backside. "And I do not lie. I cannot deny my desire for you."

As badly as he hated to admit it, his desire for her was real. He, Jamil al Hassan, who had once prided himself as being a skilled seducer before falling into this hell, had succumbed to forced seduction by a scarred woman who was a close relative to his mortal enemy.

He couldn't bring himself to call Leila's actions rape, though she had first taken him when he was chained and helpless—as certainly as her brother-by-marriage had done years earlier. And as Jamil came to know her, he could no longer consider her simply an enemy he might use to further his efforts at escape.

In her dark eyes he saw sadness. And a softness he imagined she would deny should he try to coax it from her heavily guarded soul.

But he did not see the consummate evil that lurked in the eyes of Dubaq and some of his men.

Knowing he would betray the trust she had bestowed on him filled him with guilt. He would do it, though, because he would not relinquish his only chance for life—and freedom.

Chapter Five

Jake Green couldn't begin to imagine enduring eleven years in prison, in Iraq or anywhere else. As he changed into the traditional desert robes Bear had given him along with a rundown on his plan to rescue Jamil al Hassan, he recalled the fun-loving college boy he'd partied with the week of Shana and Bear's wedding.

He wouldn't be meeting the same Jamil, that was for sure. What Jake had gone through since then had changed him, too. Most recently for the better, he thought as he bent to give his bride a farewell kiss.

Kate's eyelids fluttered. Then she looked at him with wide-eyed wonder. "What? Oh, it's you, love. I didn't recognize you at first."

"Surprised to see me dressed like a desert nomad?" he asked as he sat on the bed and laid a possessive hand over her slightly swollen belly. "You and our baby go on back to sleep, now. Bear and I are going to take a little helicopter ride."

"We're supposed to be on our honeymoon." She smiled, though, and that took the bite off her complaint.

"We are. But Bear needs to go up north, near the Iraqi border, to pick up his cousin Jamil. Since his regular pilot is on vacation, he asked me to ride up there with him in case he needs a break from flying the chopper. Let Shana and my nieces pamper you for a day or two while we're away."

"Okay." Having toured Bear's desert oilfields from the air a few days earlier, Kate wasn't anxious to ride along again on a bone-jarring helicopter to see miles and miles of endless desert where only derricks and pumpjacks dotted the barren landscape. "Go make love to your precious oil wells," she said.

"I'd rather stay here and fuck around with you." Bending, he kissed her. A long, open-mouthed kiss that made her want to strip him out of that exotic-looking garb and devour him from head to toe.

"I wouldn't go if this wasn't important. And I'll be ravenous when we get back," he said, cupping her tender breasts and tweaking the hardened nipples. "Keep the bed warm for me while I help Bear collect his cousin Jamil."

When Jake stood, the look he gave her could have set an oilfield on fire. It didn't register with Kate at first that this Jamil they were going to collect was Bear's cousin who'd been missing since the Gulf War, or that Jake might be putting himself in danger. But when she got up a few minutes later and glanced out their bedroom window, she quickly realized the situation.

What she saw on the nearby helicopter pad chilled her to the bone despite the warmth of the day. Two men loaded down with big, lethal-looking guns climbed inside the open cargo door of Bear's company chopper before the door closed and the twin rotors began to churn up sand.

May God protect them all. Fear rose in Kate's throat, threatening to choke her. Jake had tried to avoid worrying her, but it was obvious that he and Bear had just embarked on a hazardous mission to extract Bear's long-lost cousin from an Iraqi jail.

* * * * *

If Maktoum had managed to cross into Kuwait and contact Dahoud, help should already be on the way. If not…

Jamil wouldn't consider that possibility, though it was very real. In less than eight hours, he would be on his way to freedom.

Or death. But it would be better to die escaping than wait for Dubaq to do the job.

His leg irons chafed his ankles as he shuffled alongside of Brian toward the broken pump that so far had been keeping them both alive in order to repair it. "Tonight," he whispered in English, unsure whether the guard who accompanied them today could understand.

"You are certain the woman will release you from your shackles, and that you can take the key from her?" Brian asked after the guard had taken himself away to the shade of a scraggly palm tree.

Jamil shrugged. "Nothing is certain but that we will be killed if we do not escape. If all goes well, you are to subdue the guard once your chains are released. Then we will head south along the railroad track, where the old man will be waiting at the crossroad not far from the edge of the oilfield. With luck we should be able to reach the border by tomorrow evening or the next day, and my cousin will be there to meet us."

* * * * *

A few hours after they'd taken off from the villa at *Mina Su'ud,* Bear put the chopper down at the military outpost in *Abdali.* The rotors set loose sand in motion, obscuring their vision of the command center where he was to meet the messenger Maktoum.

"Good landing," Jake commented when he'd taken off his ear protectors after Bear shut down the noisy engines. "I'd hate to have had to put her down on sand the way you just did. What next?"

"We meet with Maktoum. Then we wait."

After assigning the two oilfield workers to stay and watch the chopper, Bear motioned for Jake to join him, and they headed to the nearest building, shading their eyes from the blistering sun.

While Bear spoke with Maktoum through a Kuwaiti officer who apparently understood the man's unusual dialect, Jake sipped strong, sweet coffee and stared through the window at row after row of Humvees, tanks, and other war equipment bearing the U. S. Army insignia.

He adjusted the braided band that held the *ghutra* on his head. Hell, he'd have fit right in at this particular border outpost if he'd stuck with western attire.

"Jake?"

He turned at the sound of his name. He'd never seen his easygoing brother-in-law look so fierce. "What is it?" he asked.

"Jamil has spent eleven years in hell."

The tale of horror Bear related through clenched teeth was beyond Jake's comprehension. To have been kept in a constant state of terror...

And to have watched his fellow prisoners die slowly, painfully. The sound of jailers approaching must have filled hearts with fear that they would be the ones chosen for beatings, electric shocks, amputations, castration, and rape.

The hell where Jake occasionally imagined his enemies rotting was more like paradise, compared with what Bear had just described. "I wouldn't wish that on anybody. Not even Durwood Yates," he muttered, visualizing the man who'd been caught sabotaging his company's oil wells languishing in comparatively plush surroundings of a Mississippi prison for the criminally insane.

"No one does torture quite as imaginatively as the Iraqis," Bear commented, his expression shadowed. "Only Jamil and an American pilot who will attempt escaping with him remain. Apparently the jailer, a fiend named Dubaq, has been singling prisoners out one by one for the past eleven years and torturing them to death for his twisted amusement."

Jake glanced at the Marsh Arab, then met Bear's gaze. "Are you sure he's telling you the truth?"

"Why would I doubt it? We're talking about the same Iraqi army that used prisoners of war as human shields to protect military targets. Soldiers who follow a leader who uses poison gas against his own people as well as his enemies." Bear clenched his fists. "One of the pilots in my squadron who was repatriated at the end of the Gulf War told me his captors had stuffed toilet tissue in his flight suit and set it on fire."

Jake had a sudden urge to throw up—or run for his life. A hundred miles or so was not a long enough distance to be away from demons like this jailer, to his way of thinking.

"Maktoum said Jamil has been kept alive to supervise repairs in the *Zugayr* oilfield, where the prison is located. Apparently the American was recently transferred there from another prison camp for the same purpose. Damn it, man, the bastards tortured Asad to death."

"The quiet guy who stuck with you like glue before your wedding?" Jake asked.

Bear's jaw tightened. "Yeah. The one who learned to fly jet fighters because that's what I wanted to do. If he hadn't, he might still be here today instead of being buried in that mass grave in a prison camp somewhere in the middle of *Al Zubayr.*"

"What's the plan?" Jake visualized wiping out that camp and treating the fiend who ran it to a taste of his own torture.

"They will escape after dark tonight, make their way through the desert between the railroad and the main road from Al Basrah to the border. We are to wait on this side of the border, about a mile east of the road."

"Seventy kilos is a long way to walk. Couldn't we fly inside Iraq and pick them up immediately after they escape?"

"We'd be shot down the minute we crossed the border." Bear pulled out a detailed map, pointed to a spot about three-quarters of the way from the prison to *Abdali*. "Maktoum says they will stop to rest at this oasis. If Jamil doesn't arrive at our meeting place by tomorrow night, we will head out on camelback and look for them."

Jake hated riding camels. "Why not horses?"

"Because if they don't arrive on schedule, one or both of them will most likely be hurt. Camels make better pack animals. Besides, they're what the Bedouins who live around here ride. If we rode horses, we'd attract too much attention."

* * * * *

Your scars do not repel me. I cannot hide my desire...

Jamil's declaration rang in Leila's ears as she watched Dubaq's soldiers loading equipment onto the trucks. Mernoosh had just confirmed that the troop would move out the following morning.

When she'd awakened today to the touch of Jamil's callused fingers on her undamaged cheek, she felt desirable for the first time since Saqr had left Baghdad with his Republican Guard division to try to repel the seemingly invincible American army.

For the first time since awakening in a makeshift hospital to pain and the knowledge that her beauty was gone forever, Leila had almost welcomed the light of day.

And Jamil al Hassan was the reason.

An engine coughed, then roared to life, and the troop's only battered tank lumbered up a ramp onto the biggest of the trucks, its treads making an ominous crunching sound. Apparently Dubaq intended that they travel too quickly for the tank to keep up under its own power.

Tomorrow they would leave.

And tomorrow Jamil would die.

Dubaq would shoot him and the American as though they were but pesky desert foxes. He would leave their lifeless bodies on the sand for the ever-present vultures and dung beetles to feast upon.

Sick at heart, Leila turned to the west, squinting into the afternoon sun where she sought a glimpse of Jamil in the oilfield, repairing the pump that had so far kept him and the American alive. Such a beautiful man.

A beautiful enemy.

But was he her enemy?

Jamil had done nothing to her, nothing but bring her greater sexual pleasure than she'd known for years. Once she had freed him from his shackles, he'd devoured her as though driven by his desire, not by the circumstance of his helplessness that had brought him to her.

Perhaps he had brought her the greatest pleasure of her life. And he might already have given her the son or daughter she believed would ease her awful loneliness. For that if for no other reason, Jamil did not deserve to suffer Dubaq's final vengeance.

Slowly, as though compelled by a force stronger than her own will, Leila picked up a jug of water and made her way across the desert sand.

Jamil might die, but she would not be a party to his death.

She could do no less than warn him of his intended fate. No more than offer to free him this night not so he could pleasure her but so he might make a desperate attempt at escape.

What Dubaq would surely do to her in retaliation for her part in costing him his anticipated sport did not cross Leila's mind until she overheard him gloating over his last prisoners' impending death when she passed by his and Mernoosh's bedroom as soon as darkness fell.

A sudden chill came over her. By saving her lover, she might be condemning herself to the fate from which she planned to help him escape.

Chapter Six

Leila shrugged off her fear. Surely Dubaq would not harm his wife's sister-by-marriage. It was not as though he hadn't granted her permission to loosen Jamil's chains, and he could not have been so stupid as not to have known the prisoner could physically overpower her if he so chose.

Yet deep inside she knew being the widow of Mernoosh's younger brother would not shield her from Dubaq's wrath.

She could not let that matter.

"You will wait outside," she told the beady-eyed soldier she found guarding the bunker. "I wish no prying eyes upon me this night."

Where was Maktoum? she wondered, her gaze on the soldier's worn boots as he ascended the steps. Why did Dubaq have one of his own troop guarding the prisoners tonight?

Nerves. It was only her nerves that had her on edge. Jamil was chained securely to his cot, as was the American. There was nothing different, no change in the routine that should rouse her alarm.

Quickly Leila worked the key into the locks that secured Jamil's wrists and ankles. She tried not to dwell on the fact that she would never look upon his magnificent body again. "Dubaq plans to kill you tomorrow before we leave. I cannot allow him to do so, because you have done nothing to deserve death. Go, escape now while you can. I sent the guard away, but he will be close by. Thank you for giving me pleasure." She kissed him quickly, a gesture of farewell. "Allah be with you."

Jamil slid his hand beneath her veil and caressed her cheek through the thin silk of her *hijab*. "Thank you, *houri*, but I do not go alone. Give me the key so I may free the American."

"I cannot. Dubaq will—"

"Do not make me take it from you." He held out his hand toward the pocket where she had dropped the large, heavy key.

The look on Leila's face when she laid the key in Jamil's hand bespoke pure terror. Terror he translated at once to mean fear not of him but of the retribution Dubaq was certain to take on her once he found his prisoners gone.

But his path was clear. Escape or die.

While he worked to free Shearer from his chains, Leila trembled at his side. A tear slid down her cheek and disappeared into the fabric of her scarf.

Guilt and some unfamiliar, more tender emotion assailed Jamil. "I cannot leave you to face Dubaq alone. You will come with us."

"What would become of me? I have no family, no friends in your country."

"I will take care of you."

She wiped away another tear, then looked boldly into his eyes. "I care for myself. I need no one to pity me."

"It would not be pity, but gratitude." Again Jamil was struck with that novel emotion he wasn't ready to define.

"No. Go now. I will stay and take my chances."

If she did, she would die. And Jamil wanted very much for her to live. If they abducted her...

"You will come with us if I have to knock you unconscious and carry you. Then, if we are caught, I will swear with my dying breath that we overpowered and abducted you. I cannot bear to have your torture or death at Dubaq's hands on my conscience."

Seeing that the American had finished dressing in the traditional Arab garb they wore to work outside in the desert sun, Jamil shoved Leila at him. "Hold her while I put on my robes. Do not let her go."

Leila struggled, but Shearer held her fast.

"I will scream. You will be caught and executed this night rather than on the morrow. Go, leave me in peace," she begged them.

Shearer shoved a rag into her mouth before she could follow through with her threat and slung her over his shoulder, steadying her with one hand.

"We go now. I will silence the guard." Jamil would not entrust that task to Shearer, though the sight of the American's splayed hand over Leila's nicely rounded ass evoked surprisingly possessive emotions in him.

He nearly changed his mind. But Americans were too squeamish. They would drop lethal bombs from airplanes without giving the results a second thought, but most caviled at the idea of killing an enemy up close. He imagined Brian would be even more finicky about eye-to-eye killing than most of his countrymen.

Carefully Jamil climbed the cement stairs and stepped outside. The pungent smell of a lit Turkish cigarette and a small orange glow in the darkness led his gaze to the guard. Reflected moonlight drew his eye to the Kalashnikov slung casually over the soldier's shoulder.

Good. They had not so far raised the man's suspicion. Moving silently in the shadows, Jamil approached him from behind. Less than a foot away now, he closed in, clamping his left hand over the man's open mouth while ramming the other hand upward into his nose.

Bone crunched, an eerie sound in the silence. The guard crumpled. Not daring to leave him without being certain that he could not call for help, Jamil knelt beside the body and checked for a pulse.

There was none. With his bare hands, Jamil had killed another human being. He allowed himself a moment's regret while stripping the man's rifle off his back and slinging it over his own shoulder. A quick check of the dead soldier's pockets yielded a handful of ammunition and a small but lethal looking dagger.

When he turned away, the first face he saw was Leila's. The terror he saw mirrored in her eyes made him want to comfort her, but there was no time. They had a long way to travel before morning. And a rendezvous to keep with the old man, Zayed.

Motioning for Shearer to follow with his burden, Jamil headed for the railroad tracks that would lead them to the main road between *Al Basrah* and *Al Jahrah*. The road they would follow to go home.

* * * * *

She had left her sister, the only family she had. All Leila saw of the outpost now was lights in the distance that were quickly dimming as they put distance between it and themselves with every weary step. Having been set down on her feet and ordered to keep up once they began moving along the path of the railroad tracks, she could have made a run for freedom if she'd chosen to.

Leila was confident Jamil would not kill her. After all, he had insisted she come with them to save her from Dubaq's wrath.

And the American was occupied with steadying Zayed, the frail old Marsh Arab who apparently wanted to die in freedom enough to risk this perilous journey.

Once again, she stared back at the fading lights of the compound. Had they suddenly brightened? Or was her imagination playing tricks on her?

Eyes straining in the darkness, she stared into the night. If anything, the glow was dimmer now. But what if...?

Someone might have stumbled onto the dead soldier already. If not, he and the missing prisoners would be noticed and the alarm would be raised once morning came. Looking back once more and noticing sand swirling over the path they'd traveled and obscuring their footprints, Leila realized their trail would be difficult for Dubaq to follow.

Difficult but not impossible. He would certainly guess Jamil had headed for the Kuwaiti border. Probably by the most direct route. Recalling the depths of her brother-in-law's rage when crossed, Leila was gripped with icy fear despite the warmth of the night.

Fear not so much for herself as for Jamil. And for the gnarled old *Ma'dan* who wanted freedom so desperately that he risked making this treacherous journey to escape the Marshes—a difficult undertaking for all of them, but likely impossible for him.

His labored breathing punctuated the stillness of the night.

Leila could not help but feel Zayed's pain. During his lifetime, he must have seen much sorrow. Not one loss but many, as his tribesmen had been gassed and many of the survivors dispersed. Those as stubborn as he, who had stayed and endured the tribulations, had seen their way of life erode along with the land after Saddam had ordered the Marshes drained.

When Jamil paused long enough to trade places with the American, Leila spied a lonely flower, risen out of the stark sand. A harbinger of spring. Of hope.

She dared not aspire to more than prosperity and a lonely life far from hurtful memories—yet she did. She wanted to be whole. To love and to be loved.

And she wanted the chance to know the man she'd seduced, to admire the courage and decency he'd demonstrated from the moment she set him free.

Hearing Jamil's deep, melodious voice shook her back to their most pressing issue: staying alive long enough to realize those hopes and dreams.

"Do you need a moment's rest?" he asked Zayed, who leaned heavily onto his gnarled cane when the American stepped aside so Jamil might spell him with his burden.

"No. I am slowing you enough already," the old man said, his voice no more than a raspy wheeze. "Do not concern yourself with me. When I die, my wives and sons will greet me in Paradise. And I will die happy, knowing I die free."

The American said something then in rapid English Leila could not quite make out. She did, however, follow his hand gestures toward the west, where headlights illuminated a pair of ancient trucks headed in the direction from which they had come, on what appeared to be a paved but rutted road.

"We have come farther than I'd thought," Jamil said, lengthening his stride and leading them away from the road into the shadows of a large sand dune. "*Insha'Allah*, the drivers will not have spotted us. But we must remain well away from the road."

In the moonlight, Leila saw concern in his eyes. But not fear.

After having endured years of imprisonment and torture at Dubaq's hand, he would find precious little worthy of arousing his dread. The thought of Jamil naked and chained to the dank walls like an animal awaiting mutilation and death made her shudder, even now that his chains were gone and his prison left behind in the whirling sand.

The old man's ragged breathing again pierced the silence of the desert. In the eastern sky Leila glimpsed a bit of color lightening the blanket of darkness. Day would be dawning soon, bringing with it new risks, for surely Dubaq would pursue them.

* * * * *

An oasis. Or was it a mirage?

The midday sun beat down on the weary travelers as they made their way step by step toward the border—and freedom.

Jamil pressed on, certain Dubaq and his soldiers would not be far behind. The Kalashnikov that weighed down his left shoulder would provide little protection against a pack of enraged, heavily armed fiends.

He judged they had about fifteen kilometers yet to travel before reaching Kuwait and safety. He could make it. So could Brian. But Jamil wasn't certain Leila could keep up the pace they must maintain to rendezvous with Dahoud tonight at the Kuwaiti border, and he knew the ancient Marsh Arab could not.

Though the old man plodded along, leaning on his cane and either Jamil or Brian's shoulder, Jamil saw that his strength was nearly spent. For Zayed's sake, they must stop and rest.

Perhaps they could risk an hour's respite, find fresh water to replenish their depleted supply. He weighed the danger of discovery and ambush against the risk of forging ahead and almost certainly causing the old man's death.

"We will rest there before moving on," he said, veering toward a cluster of date palms flanked by a patch of low, pale green plant growth that stood out against the desert sand.

As they approached the oasis, Jamil heard what sounded like gunshots crackling in the distance.

Chapter Seven

Hair prickled on the back of Bear's neck at the muffled sound of distant gunfire. It came not from the southwest, where his country's army was playing war games with the Americans, but from across the border somewhere in that vast sea of sand and desolation.

"Someone's shooting. That didn't come from the direction of our armies' war games," Jake said, clutching the high-powered Winchester hunting rifle he'd chosen in preference to any of the automatic combat weapons Bear had offered before they had left *Mina Su'ud*.

"I know." Sound traveled long distances over the barren desert. The shots could have been fired from as far as twenty kilos away, depending upon what kind of weapon was being fired. Fear for his cousin made Bear's stomach churn.

"Those shots could mean Jamil's in trouble," he told the others, forcing himself to remain calm.

"Let's go." Jake jerked on his camel's halter, urging the beast to its knees and clambering awkwardly into the saddle. "I've got a feeling we'd better hurry. Go, you godforsaken beast." He kicked the animal's sides, sending it loping off through the hole they'd cut in the barbed wire fence, into Iraq.

His white robe and *ghutra* flapping in the wind, Jake looked as much the desert warrior as Bear and his men, but Bear knew if Jake were captured, the Iraqis would know within moments of listening to his halting Arabic that he was a foreigner. It would take them little more effort to guess he was an American—and Bear doubted that would bode well for his brother-in-law's continued well-being.

Not that he or his men would fare much better.

Insha'Allah, they would all return unscathed from this unauthorized journey into enemy country. "Stay long enough to repair the breach in the fence," he ordered the two oilfield workers. "Then follow us." Bear lumbered across the border on his camel, keeping an eye on Jake and visually scanning the distant horizon for signs of trouble.

"Careful," he said when he caught up with his wife's impulsive brother. "This isn't Texas, my friend. Here, men shoot first and ask questions later if ever. Shana would kill me if I let anything happen to her baby brother."

"Likewise. If I let anything happen to her husband, I'd be dead meat. You take care, too. What's that?" Jake asked, gesturing toward a bird in the distance, diving straight down toward the ground.

"A kestrel. Jamil and I used to hunt with them when we were boys." Bear watched the graceful falcon swoop down, Bear assumed to pluck an unsuspecting rodent from its hiding place among some lacy desert plants.

Once, twice, three times the kestrel soared and dived.

"I've never seen one behave that way before, my sheikh," one of the men who had just caught up with them commented in Arabic when the bird made another dive, this time practically into their path. It held a writhing serpent in its beak.

Jake shook his head. "It's almost like he's trying to tell us something."

More shots rang out.

Silence followed.

Then another crack in the air. And what sounded like a woman's anguished shriek.

Ordinarily Bear didn't believe in omens. But watching the graceful raptor gave him a sense of urgency.

Those shots. The kestrel. That otherworldly shriek that sounded for all the world like a woman in the throes of grief.

And the sixth sense that told him his cousin's life was in dire peril. "The kestrel nests in the trees of the oases. Let us hurry."

By Bear's reckoning, the oasis Maktoum had mentioned yesterday lay perhaps five kilos due north, perilously close to the main highway. *Insha'Allah*, they would arrive in time, he thought as shots rang out again.

* * * * *

Leila hunkered down chin-high among tall bullrushes in the brackish water of the oasis pool where Jamil had shoved her almost as soon as the shooting had begun, as though he genuinely wanted to protect her from harm. The old man, Zayed, lay quietly at the pond's edge, his frail body partially concealed by the desert shrubs that abounded this time of year.

A kestrel dived, then soared high in a cloudless sky. The rushes shifted in the arid breeze, brushing her exposed cheek and reminding her of the scars no longer hidden by the scarf and veil she'd sacrificed to bandage the wound Dubaq's first barrage of bullets had put in the old Marsh Arab's shoulder.

Why was it so silent?

As though she had willed an end to the lull, shots rang out again. Another bullet hit the water, skimming across its surface like a lethal serpent before losing momentum and slithering into the rushes near the pond's edge.

Two men with one decent weapon now, against four fully armed soldiers. Poor odds, yet Leila held out hope that Jamil and the American would prevail. No doubt they would fight to the death to avoid the fate her brother-by-marriage had in mind for them all if they fell back into his hands.

She had witnessed the first exchange of fire and seen the methodical manner in which Jamil had aimed his weapon, dropping two approaching soldiers. The remaining three had scurried for the safety of the army truck from which Dubaq was screaming insults at them for their cowardice.

Zayed had bravely stood his ground, as well, until he'd lost too much blood from where a bullet had nicked his shoulder. The American had carried him here, asking for her scarf and veil for makeshift bandages. Now the old man lay quietly, and the American had gone back into the line of fire, brandishing Zayed's ancient weapon that was no match for the Iraqi army-issued rifles.

Leila heard more shots. Then that deafening silence that made her blood run cold.

Who was dead, and who still lived?

She dared not move, lest a soldier discover her and shoot.

But she needed to know. Had Dubaq slaughtered her lover?

Her *yoni* clenched when she thought of Jamil as she had seen him these past hours, proud, strong, and free from the chains that had confined his body but not his will. A warrior prince, no longer a prisoner.

No more a helpless pawn who must do her sexual bidding. But a man. A man who would bend her to his stronger will. A lover who would take her of his own volition as she had taken him, in a haze of sexual need.

Perhaps he did desire her. He could not have hated her, or he would have confined her in the bunker to face Dubaq's fury. Wouldn't he?

Foolish woman. Jamil may not hate you. He will keep his word, take care of you in the land to which we travel. But remember how you look, and accept that he will never care for you the way a man desires a woman.

Leila's hand went to her cheek, and she caressed the rough scarred flesh no man could want to touch.

Another shot rang out, its report lacking the hollow sound of metal passing through air. Then silence reigned again but for the squawk of another diving desert falcon and the labored breathing of the old Marsh Arab. When she looked his way, she saw his blood had soaked through the *shaila* the American had quickly bound around his wounded shoulder.

At the sound of footsteps, Leila dipped her head under the water.

And realized that when she came up for air, either Jamil, the American, or Dubaq and his remaining soldiers would see her shame.

"Zayed's still breathing, but he's lost a lot of blood."

Jamil glanced at Brian, who had knelt beside the old man and proceeded to tend his wound. Then he peered into the shallow pool. *Insha'Allah*, no bullet had found Leila.

Fear gripped him when he didn't see her immediately among the rushes where he had ordered her to hide. But then she surfaced, her expression anguished when she briefly met his gaze.

Her hands went to her ruined cheek as though to hide it, and she bowed her bare head. "Dubaq?"

"I gave him a more humane death than he accorded my countrymen."

Leila met his gaze, then quickly bowed her head as though she had suddenly remembered again that he could see her scars. "You shot him?"

"We both did. After his two remaining men fled, he charged us, though he already carried my bullet in his shoulder. Brian took him down with the old man's gun. I slit his throat."

"Did ending his life give you pleasure?"

"No. The revenge would have been sweeter had I left him there to die in his own time." Jamil wished she would look at him, because from her calm, uncharacteristically restrained tone he could read nothing of her reaction.

The temptation had been strong for him to abandon the evil commander to die slowly or be eaten alive by desert scavengers. But in the final moment, Jamil learned he had not the stomach for meting out the sort of torture Dubaq had inflicted with such glee. "I do not gain the sort of pleasure your brother-by-marriage apparently derived from inflicting pain on others."

"Then you will do me the courtesy of averting your eyes while I retrieve my veil."

Jamil held out his hand. "Come. We must move on, in case Dubaq sent for more soldiers once it became evident the ones he had with him would not succeed in killing us. Your scars do not repel me," he said softly. "I, too, have vulnerabilities, although most of mine aren't visible to the human eye. The old man, Zayed, has need of the garments you like to hide behind."

Though Leila took his hand and let him lift her from the pool, she did her best to cover the scarred side of her face and head from Jamil's gaze. The side he saw clearly made him realize she had once been an extraordinary beauty, with flawless olive skin and delicately hewn cheekbones. Short, glossy sable hair curved smoothly around the delicate shell of her ear.

It was not the disfiguring scars she tried to hide that attracted Jamil's eye, but the sleek curves covered but not concealed by her sopping wet tunic.

They had escaped from hell and fought the devil himself. And for the moment they all still lived. Something primitive within Jamil rose, urging him to celebrate life, to take this prideful woman under the desert sun and stake his claim.

"Jamil. I must tend the old man's wound. To move him now would kill him," Brian said quietly.

"We have no choice."

Brian looked at Zayed, his expression somber. "I will not leave him, and he is not fit to travel. If I can get the bleeding stopped—"

"We will rest for an hour. No more. We cannot if we are to reach the border by nightfall. Meanwhile we have more to concern ourselves with than the old man." When Jamil saw Brian start to remove his *ghutra*, he snatched off his own. "Here, take mine to use for bandaging. Keep yours on your head. Without it, even the most isolated of nomads would recognize you as a foreigner."

"Nomads?"

"A band approaches from the south. From the dust cloud I see, I judge it's a small camel caravan. If we are lucky, they will seek the water in that larger pond and not notice our presence. If they confront us, do not speak. I will try to avert them."

While the camel drivers might guess Jamil wasn't a native Iraqi, they certainly would realize immediately if Brian spoke that he was not. And Jamil had no intention of exposing Leila if he could prevent it. Only Allah knew how long it might have been since the nomads had been with their women.

"Get back among the rushes," he told her.

Zayed moaned, and Leila hunkered back down into the shadows provided by the tall rushes on the shoreline.

Shading his eyes from the fierce sun with one hand, Jamil peered at the dust cloud, making out the shapes of three, no four camels, and then their riders as the caravan came closer.

Robed men. Four of them. Jamil cautioned the others that the strangers were nearing the oasis. "Be silent."

The sound of metal hitting metal reverberated when he filled a clip with the last of the ammunition he'd taken from the soldier he'd killed and inserted it into the Kalashnikov. A water bird squawked, then hit the water of the larger pond with a jarring splash.

"Jamil?" Leila rested her hand tentatively on Jamil's shoulder.

"Come. We will conceal ourselves amidst these rushes." The nomads obviously had spotted the Iraqi army truck and were steering clear of it.

Unfortunately that meant the band would pass dangerously close to their hiding place on their way to the oasis.

"Jamil. The men on those camels are loaded for bear," Brian said as he hunkered down low, as though to shield the old man from harm.

When Jamil glanced toward the approaching nomads, the glint of the noonday sun on four shiny automatic weapons nearly blinded him.

With just one weapon and a single clip of bullets, they'd be no match for the heavily armed band.

Insha'Allah, the nomads would hold no love for the fallen soldiers.

* * * * *

A water bird soared skyward from a pond in the oasis, apparently frightened by something from its search for food and water. Silence, ominous in the wake of what obviously had been a gun battle, weighed heavily on Jake's ears.

Wanting to disperse the unease that had settled over him, he scanned the desert topography seeking hints of where black gold might lie beneath glistening hot sand. "Over there," he told Bear when he spotted a brackish pond surrounded by scraggly rushes. "A thousand says we'd find oil if we drilled, say twenty feet north-northwest of that little pond."

"Since this piece of real estate is in Iraq, I doubt we'll be able to test your hunch. " Bear paused, squinting in the direction of the oasis. "See the GAZ?" he asked.

Using his hand to shade his eyes, Jake made out the basic shape of a canvas-topped vehicle on the other side of the pond. "Looks like some kind of truck. What the hell is a GAZ?"

"An army personnel carrier. Soviet era. The Iraqis still use them. Be prepared to shoot." Bear repeated the order in Arabic to their two companions.

Jake resisted the urge to gallop in as fast as the miserable beast he was riding could go. He had Kate now, and their baby on the way. He couldn't go headlong into danger any more. He had too much to live for.

Expecting to be welcomed with a barrage of bullets at any second, he found the continued silence anticlimactic. Then he saw the bodies.

"I count five," he told Bear. "Looks like they're wearing army uniforms."

"Yeah. Careful. Some of them may still be alive." Bear shifted his weapon to his left hand and tugged at his camel's reins. "They must have come after Jamil."

Whatever Bear snarled in Arabic got his camel moving so fast that it drew away from Jake and the others.

Jake had to keep up, watch Bear's back to keep him from getting himself killed in the process of rescuing Jamil. When swearing in English didn't seem to have the desired effect on his own camel, he drew on his very limited Arabic vocabulary. "Go, you flea-bitten beast," he yelled, accompanying the command with a swift kick to the dromedary's sides.

Their robes and *ghutras* flapping in the wind, the four men charged toward the oasis, past the remains of five men in fatigues. Iraqi soldiers, Jake knew for sure as soon as he spotted the distinctive insignia on the sleeves of the jackets.

Another body lay a little closer to the oasis. This one apparently was an officer. And he sure as hell was dead. Blood stained the sand from a huge gash in his throat and what looked like gunshot wounds to his gut and right shoulder.

When they approached the brackish pond, Jake spied two men in traditional Arab garb, one apparently tending the other's wounds.

And he saw Bear, urging his camel to its knees at the water's edge.

When his own mount knelt, Jake struggled out of the oddly shaped saddle and ran to his brother-in-law's side, leaving the injured man and his tender to the two burly oilfield workers.

If Bear hadn't been hugging the gaunt man with a recently shaved head, Jake doubted he would have recognized Jamil. He looked nothing like the jovial Kuwaiti student he remembered from years ago when they'd partied in Houston before Bear and Shana's wedding. No wonder, Jake told himself. After all, Jamil had spent the past eleven years in hell.

Despite his initial shock at Jamil's appearance, Jake couldn't help noticing the angry burn scars Jamil's female companion was apparently trying to hide by splaying her fingers across her ravaged cheek. The incredible beauty of the uninjured side of her face stood out in such stark contrast, it was all he could do to squelch an anguished cry.

What a desolate place this must be, for people to let injuries like hers go untreated. At home they'd pull out all the stops for her. No doubt his mother knew half a dozen cosmetic surgeons who'd…hell, Shana most likely had her own private youth-preserver in Kuwait City. Maybe even in *Mina Su'ud*.

Chapter Eight

The gazes of Jamil's cousin and his American brother-by-marriage seared Leila's skin like a fiery brand. Though she realized the effort was futile, she lowered her head, tugging the neckline of her tunic as high on her neck as it would go.

What she would have given at this moment for an all-encompassing *abaya*. She'd even have worn the sort of *burqa* that would have hidden all her features from the men's disbelieving stares—if only she had one.

Hard to believe she'd once pitied school friends whose families insisted they hold fast to the old tradition of *hijab*.

"They do not know your inner beauty as I do," Jamil whispered as they made their way toward Brian and the old Marsh Arab. "Or the pleasures I have discovered in your embrace."

"And they will not. The way your American kinsman looked at me, I thought he surely would bolt and run." Trying not to dwell on the fact that Jamil seemed to know what she was thinking when she hadn't voiced her discomfort, Leila reached up and ran her fingers through hair she'd kept short since she'd lost most of it in the fire so long ago. The sun beat down on skin she hadn't bared to it for eleven long years. "Are we in Kuwait now?"

"No. But we are close." Jamil gestured toward his kinsmen. "Brian, these are my cousin Dahoud and his wife's brother Jake, and the nomads with the guns trained on you are Dahoud's men. They mean you no harm," he called out when they approached, his English apparently as fluent as the Arabic he'd always spoken to her.

Then he wrapped his arm about her shoulders. More than his soothing words, the protective gesture brought home to Leila that Jamil understood her embarrassment and wished to put her at ease.

If only that were possible.

"Moving Zayed now would kill him," Brian protested when Jamil said they'd have to make haste lest more of Dubaq's men should come. "I will not leave him to face them alone."

"If more soldiers come, they will kill us all. The old man will have the help he needs as soon as we reach *Abdali*." The man who was Jamil's cousin had a deep, booming voice. It fit well with his great height and broad shoulders. Jamil's English was fluent, but Dahoud spoke it as easily if he used the language every day. Perhaps he did. After all, his wife must be an American since her brother Jake obviously was.

"Leave me. I will die free, here in the desert." Zayed's voice rang out strongly, considering how much of his blood had already soaked through the layers of makeshift bandages that Brian held firmly against his shoulder.

"No."

Jake knelt beside Brian and looked the old man over as though he was assessing Zayed's condition. Then he looked up at Jamil. "Will that army truck run?"

"As far as I know. We didn't have enough ammunition to waste by aiming for the petrol tank." Jamil paused. "Obviously we could not risk driving it along the road."

Dahoud glanced at the truck, then at one of his men. "Go get it. If it gets stuck here, where the sand is damp, then we will know we cannot take it all the way to the border. If not, we'll load Brian and the old man up and lead the way on the camels."

A few minutes later, Jamil lifted Leila into the saddle of Jake's camel and mounted behind her. If the situation had not been so tense, she would have laughed at the speed with which Jake had volunteered to drive the truck while the American prisoner tended Zayed's wounds in the back. Apparently he was unimpressed with camels as a means of transportation.

"Will we pass by Dubaq's body?" she asked once the camel was on its feet and moving slowly in the direction of Kuwait.

"No. I am sorry I had to deprive your sister of her husband. But he left me with no choice unless I wanted to be the one to die."

For a moment Leila grieved for Mernoosh's loss. Then she recalled how Saqr's sister had married Dubaq eleven years ago within days of her first husband's death on the battlefield. She would soon find another soldier to warm her bed.

"Dubaq was an evil man who caused many to die. He deserved his fate. My sister-by-marriage will survive. She always does."

* * * * *

By sunset, they had crossed the border into Kuwait, and in another hour Jamil found himself taking the first hot shower he'd enjoyed for more than eleven years. *Abdali* was busier than he remembered, a bustling town hosting not only a division of the Kuwaiti army but also a huge contingent of American soldiers. Apparently they were engaged in mock desert war games in the shadow of the Iraqi border.

Brian had stayed at the army base infirmary with Zayed, saying he would join them at the hotel once the old man was reunited with his grandson. After dropping Jamil and Leila off here, Dahoud and Jake had gone with Dahoud's men to prepare for their return to *Mina Su'ud* on the morrow.

Dahoud had apologized for accommodations that seemed grand now but which Jamil realized he'd have scoffed at before his imprisonment. Now, though, the modest hotel provided everything he required: hot water, soap, razor, toothbrush, a comfortable bed—and Leila in the adjoining room.

Jamil had come too near to death not to want to celebrate life. And who better to celebrate it with than the woman who had helped him escape from hell? The one he had promised to care for in this land full of people she'd been conditioned since childhood to hate.

Insha'Allah, she would want to cast her lot with him. His cock reared up against his belly when he thought of turning the tables, fucking her so long and so well she could have no doubt about his desire.

Or his gratitude, for without her help he never would have escaped from hell.

If nothing else, his proposal of marriage should convince Leila he was sincere.

He stepped out of the shower and dried himself before using the towel to wipe the steam off the first mirror he'd seen in more than eleven years. When he glanced in it to wield the disposable razor he'd found on a plastic soap dish, a gaunt stranger with three days' growth of beard and the remnants of a recently shaved head stared him in the face. He bore no resemblance to the dark-haired, smiling young pilot he'd been before his capture.

Staring at himself while he scraped off the stubble from his chin, Jamil realized the changes inside him outweighed the outward signs of his ordeal. Before, he would have laughed at any suggestion that he might find a scarred Iraqi woman attractive. Of course he'd also have scoffed at the idea of succumbing to such a woman's forced seduction.

Now he could barely wait to cross that hotel room, open the adjoining door, and take his fill of Leila—his way this time. Stopping first to slip a clean *dishdasha* over his head, he rapped on the door between their rooms.

The woman who answered the door was traditionally garbed for out-of-doors, including a *burqa* that completely obscured her features.

"Leila?"

"It is I."

"Welcome to Kuwait. Whatever you may have heard, we do not require *hijab* of our women. Only our neighbors to the south insist upon it, and even they do not go so far as to require *burqas* like that one. Besides, I have no plan for us to leave the privacy of our rooms this night."

"I have no desire to venture outside. But I wish to shield my scars from pitying stares."

"By doing so, *houri*, you also obscure your beauty from my eyes." Jamil slid his hands under the *burqa* and rested them on Leila's trembling shoulders. "Take it off or I will do it for you. Note that I am no longer chained, no longer your prisoner. I would prove to you what I said when I was shackled and helpless. Your scars do not repel me."

Slowly Leila lifted her arms, grasped the coarse material of the *burqa*, and lifted it over her bowed head. When Jamil lifted her chin and looked into her deep brown eyes, he saw stubborn pride—and fear.

"I will care for you as I promised, Leila. As soon as I can arrange it, I will make you my wife. And if I still have wealth, I will see what can be done toward restoring what my eyes tell me was once beauty almost beyond belief. For your sake, because to me you are beautiful as you are today." He stroked her unscarred cheek, ran his fingers through thick, lustrous hair that felt like a velvety pelt above the perfect shell of her ear. "Now, *houri*, I would examine what will be mine."

"You wish us to marry?"

"Who better than you to become the bride of a man who has gone through hell? What woman might understand as fully when I do not laugh and joke and devote myself to the life of pleasure I enjoyed before enduring the years of humiliation Dubaq inflicted on me? I cannot imagine a woman better equipped to bridge the gap between the good life I can barely remember and the hell I will never be able to forget."

She didn't stop him when he slid the black *abaya* off her shoulders and draped it across a chair. But when he bent to lift her tunic, she stepped back until the bed blocked her escape. "These scars are not my only ones," she said, her voice flat.

"I did not imagine they were. Remove the tunic, Leila."

As though fear paralyzed her, she stood there. The tears sliding down her cheeks, their paths uneven over satin-smooth skin on one side, scar tissue on the other, provided the only motion to an otherwise frozen scene.

"Take it off." With the terse command, Jamil moved close enough that he could enfold her in his arms.

Suddenly she did as he commanded, but she dived beneath the covers on the narrow bed before Jamil could get a good look at the body he had already explored by touch through the concealing fabric of the her tunic.

Furious because he wanted her to bare herself freely to him, he grabbed the *burqa* and ripped it into four long strips. Leaving her covered while he used the remnants of the garment to tie her arms and legs to the four corners of the bed, Jamil tried to rein in conflicting emotions that assailed him.

Anger at the ravages war had left them with. Fear for a future in a world neither of them had seen for years. Lust, he thought, as his balls tightened in their sac at the sight of her squirming against her bonds. And something more. Hope for their future happiness that was no longer a futile fantasy.

Jamil snatched off his *dishdasha* and tossed it away. "Look on me now. You have seen before, but now I show you freely what war and imprisonment have done to me. There is more you cannot see with your eyes that you will learn in time from witnessing my nightmares. Now I would see the body I've mated with in the darkness. I would feast my eyes upon your *yoni*. Your full, soft breasts."

When he pulled back the covers, they caught briefly on the chain she wore between her nipple rings, making her nipples grow hard and tight. Even before he settled between her legs and caught her clitoris between his teeth, her *yoni* was wet for him.

Until she felt the warmth of his seeking fingers on her left breast, she'd almost forgotten her disfigurement. The lack of sensation when he touched the rough, hardened scar tissue there brought home the fact that she would never be whole again.

"No," she whispered, tugging in vain to free her wrists from their bonds.

Raising his head, he cupped both of her breasts in his hands and gently tugged at the rings in her nipples. "Yes. I give thanks to Allah for sparing these. One day they will nurture my child."

He truly meant to make her his wife?

Leila quit fighting the bonds that grew tighter on her wrists and ankles with every desperate attempt at escape. It mattered not, now that Jamil had seen each puckered scar, every shiny surface where the doctors had grafted skin to replace what the fireball that followed that terrifying explosion of an enemy bomb had destroyed.

A bomb dropped by his allies if not by Jamil himself had done this to her, she thought even as she grew hotter and wetter with every stroke of his callused fingers on her breasts, her belly, the sensitive skin of her widespread inner thighs. On her *yoni*, open and vulnerable to serve his pleasure.

"So soft," he murmured, his smoothly shaven cheek against her belly while he toyed with the chain that joined her nipples and the ring in her navel. "This night I will take you as you took me when I was bound, and if Allah wills it, you will bear my child by the time that ten new moons have come and gone."

Her mouth watered to taste his rigid *lingam*, and she wanted her hands free not to flee but to press his smoothly shaven face between her legs. To stroke the silky, jet black stubble that was already beginning to form a short pelt on his beautifully shaped head.

"Come to me, my sheikh. I would take your magnificent *lingam* inside my *yoni* and milk it dry."

He sat upright, his dark eyes aglow with desire. The broad head of his penis glistened on its rigid shaft, hot and pulsating as though it had a life of its own.

Leaning toward her, he bent until his breath ruffled her ruined hair. "Dahoud assures me my family's possessions are now mine, so I can promise you some degree of financial security, though it may not amount to the wealth we had before the invasion. I doubt I will ever fully recover mentally from the effects of my imprisonment, any more than your scars will suddenly fade away. Or that I will soon become accustomed again to being called 'sheikh' instead of 'prisoner.'"

"I care not. I hurt with wanting you."

"Say you will wed with me, Leila. Say it now and I will give you what you want." He reached down, rubbed his steely erection against her belly. "I will give you this."

"If you will allow me *hijab*, I will marry you." Surely he would take another wife to display before his friends and family. And to take to his bed once he shook off the worst effects of his imprisonment. That realization hurt, but she dared not try to extract the promise from Jamil that Saqr had reluctantly made her so long ago: that he would take her as his only wife.

"You may hide yourself from others if that is your wish, *houri*, but you must never shrink away from me. I would have you naked in my bed, in the light of day as well as under cover of darkness."

He stroked her scarred cheek, then tunneled his fingers into her hair that had never grown back properly after having been burned away. "These are nothing compared to my scars. You may not see them but they are alive inside me. Scars of humiliation. Memories of being chained and raped like a whore by Dubaq and his men. Of watching my countrymen endure similar torture only to be maimed and killed one by one as it served our captors' pleasure.

"You brought me pleasure, though you gave me no choice. Now I would prove you need not shrink away from the light. Feel my desire and know it is real."

Like velvet over steel, his long, thick *lingam* pulsed against the naked flesh of her belly. In his dark eyes she saw passion's fire. Her body answered his call with a fresh gush of hot, slippery lubrication that dripped from her *yoni* and settled around the entrance to her rear passage.

"I will wed with you, my sheikh," she said, desperate now for him to ease the ache that began in her puckered nipples and settled deep within her body. "Fuck me now. Do not make me wait."

In one smooth motion, he sat on his haunches between her legs and filled her. Hot. Thick. Incredibly beautiful because this time Jamil was fucking her because he wanted her. He might not love her—most certainly he did not—but Leila could not refute the desire that was evident in his pulsing erection that stretched the walls of her vagina.

Lifting her hips, straining against bonds far more gentle than the heavy chains Dubaq had ordered used on him each night, she felt her own passion build with every thrust and parry, each slide of his callused fingertips across the jutting points of her nipples.

His gaze was hot, dark, locked with her own when he seated himself in her so deep that his satiny balls rested against the sensitive entrance to her anus. His obsidian gaze held hers, and his hands slid down her body, gently tugging at the thin chains and tweaking her nipples as they moved.

When he found the hot, hard nub of her clitoris and rubbed it between his thumb and forefinger, she gasped with the exquisite pleasure and clenched her inner muscles harder around his invading *lingam*.

"I've never met a more responsive woman," he said, catching both of the chains where they converged at her navel ring and jiggling them to stimulate her nipples while he did his magic between her legs. "I will have your nipple rings chained to this," he told her as he gave her stiff little clitoris a quick, arousing pinch.

The thought of constantly stimulating the jewel of her sex made her clench her *yoni* harder around him. "And how would you decorate my navel, my sheikh?"

"I'll buy you jewels to adorn it, a precious stone for each day of the week. And you will dance for me in the privacy of our rooms." He thrust into her harder, deeper, each time withdrawing almost completely before filling her again.

The first waves of her climax rippled deep in her belly, radiating through her body like the fire that had practically destroyed her. It went on for what seemed like forever, consuming her so thoroughly she didn't realize until he clasped her hands and dragged them to rest on his heaving chest that he had freed her from her bonds.

Holding back his own release when Leila's pussy squeezed his cock like a greedy fist had Jamil trembling. When she scissored her fingers over the sensitive nubs of his nipples, he almost exploded.

"No, *houri*. I would give you more pleasure before I spend." Slowly, he withdrew from her hot, wet pussy and released her legs, kissing his way up the silky flesh from ankle to thigh, then tasting her satiny *yoni* with long, lazy strokes of his tongue while he pulled on the golden chain that connected her pink, pebbled nipples.

She smelled like apricots and spices and female musk, and he couldn't get enough of her essence. But his cock ached to feel her pussy around it, hot and tight, so much that prolonging the pleasure like this could not last for long.

Gently he turned her on her stomach and knelt between her legs, spreading her and raising her sweet ass for his attention. Her puckered anus twitched when he ringed it with his finger after moistening it with her own slick juices.

She opened further to him, lifting her ass as though she liked him touching her there. "Oh, yesss."

Her husky purr resonating in his ears, he inserted a finger past her anal sphincter, taking care not to cause her the pain he'd always associate with the act she seemed to want.

"Do you want me to fuck you here?" he asked when she moaned again.

"Someday. But not now. I want your big, thick *lingam* in my *yoni*. Now."

Jamil shifted, found her sweet *yoni* and sank slowly inside until his balls pressed hard against her clit. It felt like paradise, having her pulsating around his cock like this.

"Lock your ankles around my ass," he said, lifting her lower body as he rose to his knees.

"Like this?"

With her back arched sweetly into his belly and her face and upper body pressed against the snowy bed linen, Jamil saw none of the devastation Leila wanted so badly to hide. Her rounded ass and sleek back, even the silky hair on the back of her shapely head showed him only perfect womanly beauty.

"By Allah, yes." He could barely hold in his seed when she pulled him in her so deep that his cock pressed at the entrance to her womb. But he wanted her to come again, too.

Very gently he worked first one, then another finger into her rear passage and began to slide them in and out. Her pussy clenched him like a fist, and her slick, hot juices bathed his balls in liquid heat.

His cock swelled against the sweet constriction of her vaginal muscles, and the first waves of orgasm shot from his belly to his balls. He was losing control. While he finger-fucked her ass faster and harder, he reached beneath her, found the love chain, and tugged it to stimulate her nipples.

"Oh, yesss. Don't stop. I..." Whatever she was going to say was lost in her ecstatic scream. A scream that pushed Jamil over the edge and triggered the wild, hot spurts of semen that shot into her convulsing pussy.

Chapter Nine

While Jamil slept in Leila's arms, Brian sat at the unconscious Marsh Arab's bedside even after Zayed's grandson had arrived.

As anxious as he was to get processed at the American Air Force base in Saudi Arabia and fly home to Diane, Brian felt compelled to stay. It was as though Zayed had somehow become part of him during their flight.

"He stepped in front of a bullet that was meant for me," he'd told the old man's grandson in halting Arabic when Maktoum asked why he didn't leave and get his own rest.

Maktoum had nodded, as though he understood. "He is a Wise One."

What that meant, Brian hadn't a clue. But he passed the night swabbing sweat off Zayed's brow, hoping the old man would live while knowing from some spot deep inside him that the wound had been too much for the ninety-year-old man to survive.

How he knew, he could not explain. Both the Kuwaiti doctor and the American specialist Jake summoned had given Maktoum an optimistic prognosis for his grandfather.

But he knew with certainty that Zayed would not last the night. And that he had somehow willed him, Brian, to keep a death watch.

Outside the wind howled. Through the window of the old man's hospital room, Brian watched the swirling sand create a macabre moving picture in the light of the new moon.

Zayed stirred, as though roused by nature's unrest beyond these walls. With one bony hand, he reached to his chest and clasped the strange necklace Brian had first noticed this afternoon while he tended the old man's wound.

"May I help you?" Maktoum asked, and when the old man nodded, he unclasped the necklace and placed it in his grandfather's hand.

With what seemed like superhuman effort, Zayed lifted his hand and placed the necklace into Brian's hand. "Take this, young man. You will need—"

The Marsh Arab's strange dialect and his rapid, breathy speech over what sounded like death rattles was too much for Brian to translate any more of what Zayed was trying to say. But he gathered that the old man wanted him to have the necklace.

"He wants you to take it, says you will need it to show you the way to paradise," Maktoum told Brian after Zayed had lapsed into unconsciousness.

An hour later, with his grandson holding one bony hand and Brian clasping the other, the old man died.

* * * * *

Their ordeal was over. Jamil was home at last.

Well, not home, because the Iraqi army had destroyed his childhood home and killed his immediate family during the invasion years ago. But they'd arrived two days earlier at his cousin's villa near *Mina Su'ud*, the one he'd built after the one Jamil remembered had been destroyed during the Iraqi invasion. And yesterday Dahoud and Jake had taken him by helicopter to view his own oilfields that were now almost back at full production thanks to eleven years' hard work by the GreenTex crews Dahoud had hired to tend them after the war was over.

He'd learned how Jake had supervised much of the rebuilding after he graduated from college and took his place with his family's company. And that Jake was here now not to work but to enjoy an extended honeymoon with his new bride.

Much had happened to his cousin during the years of Jamil's imprisonment. Yet one thing remained the same. Dahoud and his beautiful American still showed every sign of being madly, wildly in love.

The reunion had been sweet. Seeing Dahoud's daughters and infant son made Jamil anxious to start living again, build a home for himself and Leila and start their own family. Tomorrow Dahoud's parents and his sister Alina would arrive from Kuwait City to celebrate his escape—and his marriage.

The rich fabric of Dahoud's traditional robe and headdress that he had borrowed felt strange after his years in rough prison garb and the time before that when he had eschewed tradition in favor of Western clothing. Since Leila wished to hide her disfigurement beneath traditional *hijab*, though, he thought he should dress to match.

After their wedding, which Dahoud's wife Shana was already planning with unseemly glee, Jamil would take Leila to the States to see renowned plastic surgeon Brent d'Angelo. Shana said he'd done her mother's facelift as well as those for dozens of Hollywood celebrities and political personalities. Apparently he'd also performed liposuction on two Saudi princesses of their acquaintance, a fact which seemed to amuse his gorgeous cousin-by-marriage when she divulged it.

Insha'Allah, the man would be able to erase the worst of Leila's scars. For himself, he cared not. To Jamil, she was beautiful and desirable the way she was, and he thought he'd done a good job of proving that to her since regaining his freedom three days earlier.

"Are you ready, *houri*?" he called through the door, amused to have been banned while she dressed after they had worshiped each other's naked bodies for hours the night before.

"I am now."

Jamil liked Shana's idea of *hijab*. The ruby-red tunic his cousin's wife had loaned Leila clung to her supple curves, and a sheer scarf in a pattern of rose and red and gold shimmered about her face and neck and chin, calling attention to her incredibly sexy eyes, shapely nose, and the rosy full lips that had wakened him so lovingly this morning when they slid down his sleepy cock.

Shana el Rashid was an incredibly sexy lady. And so was Jake's bride Kate, in her own quiet way. But neither of them got him instantly hot and hard the way Leila did.

"You look beautiful," he told her, thinking that if he said it often enough when his cock wasn't reaming her pussy or buried down her throat, she'd come to believe him.

"Thank you. We should go and say good-bye to Brian."

"We should be seeing him again soon. He has accepted the job Jake offered him with GreenTex Petroleum. From what Dahoud said last night, the company manages several oilfields in Kuwait and Saudi Arabia. Because Brian speaks a little Arabic, I imagine he will be assigned to work here often."

* * * * *

The expansive living room they entered moments later still took Leila's breath away. An eclectic mix of old and new, east and west, it faced the *Khalij*, or Persian Gulf as Jake and Brian called it. This morning the first thing she spied when she looked out over the water was a huge ship in the distance, with gleaming silver airplanes on its deck.

She couldn't help staring at it, even when Jake's pregnant wife Kate came up beside her.

"That's the *George Washington*," Kate told her. "Funny, the carriers hardly ever come so close to shore. Of course, these are friendly waters," she added, apparently not wanting to offend anyone with her observation.

Leila shuddered, for she understood Kate's American pride even though most of the words were beyond her comprehension. She also knew firsthand the peril regimes faced when they incurred the fury of the American military machine.

She'd been conditioned since childhood to believe in Iraq. In Saddam, for whom her father fought and died. But at that prison outpost her vicious brother-by-marriage had operated in the name of his leader, Leila had seen the incredible cruelty of some Iraqi soldiers. She'd witnessed the result of Saddam's disregard for the Iraqi people after he had drained the marshes and destroyed the livelihood of good Iraqis like Maktoum and Zayed, who had risked his life in order to die free.

"I hope a peaceful solution may be found," she said, though she was fairly certain Kate understood very little Arabic.

"I do, as well," Kate said, and she clasped Leila's hand.

A feeling of goodwill washed over her. Perhaps Kate had grasped some of what she had said, the way Leila herself comprehended a few words of English.

"Leila, come see this," Dahoud bellowed from across the room where the men had congregated.

"What, my lord Dahoud?"

"The eye Brian holds here in his hand. The old Marsh Arab gave it to him before he died. I have seen nothing like it, and neither has Jamil. Have you?"

Standing close to Jamil, enjoying the security of his presence, Leila looked at the odd, ancient-looking center stone that was painted to resemble a clear, blue human eye. An eye that bore a single tear. Its filigree setting was made of pure gold, and three glittering, multifaceted ruby-colored stones hung at the bottom of the setting, suspended on finely wrought gold chains.

Were it not for the workmanship and the obvious value, Leila might have mistaken the necklace for the sort of pagan talismans hawkers used to sell in the bazaars of Baghdad. "No, I have never seen anything like this before. May I hold it for a moment?"

Brian passed over the necklace, and when it touched Leila's hand it seemed that the tear she saw had vanished. She must have been mistaken about that, though, for when she gave it back to Brian and took another look, the glittering tear was still there.

But there was something strange about the piece, something that made Leila shiver. It was as though it carried with it the spirit of people whose lives had touched it through the ages. She clasped Jamil's hand a little tighter.

"Mahmoud told me Zayed found it when he was a young man, fishing for his livelihood," Brian said. "It apparently had become tangled in the rushes near the convergence of the Tigris and Euphrates Rivers. Of course that was years ago, before the Butcher of Baghdad drained the marshes." Jamil paused and squeezed Leila's hand again, as if to reassure her. Had he seen the tear disappear, too? Or was he simply reacting to her concern?

"Well, Brian, I wouldn't lose any sleep over it if I were you. Consider it a good luck charm. Come on, I've got clearance to fly you down to the Prince Sultan Airbase so you can get started bringing yourself back to life with the Air Force and getting discharged," Jake said, picking up a brown leather briefcase and striding toward his bride.

Today Jake looked the part of the American cowboy in jeans and boots. But Leila got the impression he was almost as comfortable wearing the desert robes he'd had on when he and Dahoud had charged in on camels to rescue them at an Iraqi oasis.

Well, maybe Jake wasn't all that comfortable riding camels, she amended when she recalled how quickly he'd volunteered to drive the army truck and let her and Jamil ride on his "miserable beast." But she had no trouble picturing him galloping across the desert on one of Dahoud's sleek Arabian stallions, white robes flapping in the wind.

He wasn't the monster she'd grown up thinking all Americans must be. Neither was Brian or Kate. Or beautiful, sensual Shana, whose love for Dahoud showed in her every graceful motion, in each detail of the beautiful home they'd built after the retreating Iraqi army had destroyed the old el Rashid villa during the war.

"Allah go with you, Brian. We look forward to meeting your wife when we visit next month in America," Jamil said, giving the American a quick hug. As they watched Brian leave with Jake and Kate, Leila sensed some impending sorrow, but she quickly banished it. Life today was good. What would be, would be.

* * * * *

That night three pairs of lovers looked out over the *Khalij* from their private quarters in Bear's palatial villa.

Bear stood behind Shana, nibbling at the sensitive spot he'd recently found behind one ear while he played with the pointed nubs of her nipples. He loved the way they jutted so proudly forward, the jewels in her nipple shields reflecting blue fire from the light of fragrant candles flickering in the breeze. His cock swelled more with every moment he denied it its rightful place in her hot, tight pussy, nudging her back until she turned and led him to the silken couch where she once again became his wanton harem love slave.

In one of the guest suites, Jake held Kate on his lap on a lounge chair beside their bedroom door after they'd made love and cradled her expanding belly in both hands, thanking God he'd found her. Soon they'd go home to Texas, to his job and their everyday life. Damn, he pitied Brian. Eleven years away from the woman he loved would have killed him, yet Brian seemed to have survived. Now, under the light of a moon reflecting on a carrier in the Persian Gulf, Jake stroked his wife's satiny skin as they basked in the afterglow.Next door Jamil held Leila in his arms while he looked out over the *Khalij* at the ships' lights from an American carrier group. A presence that augured war. Despite them, Jamil felt at peace tonight, for he had been granted not only freedom but love. For the first time in years, he felt he might someday find remnants in himself of the exuberant young man who long ago had embarked upon another war with the same enemy Kuwait might enjoin again, side by side with its invincible American ally.

Tonight, though, being here with Leila satisfied all his needs. "I love you," he whispered against her hair, suddenly aware of the emotions that had risen soon after she'd seduced him and lurked below the surface of his consciousness until now.

"And I love you, my sheikh," she replied, tilting her head back and seeking his descending lips. "*Nek ni.*"

"Fucking you will be my greatest pleasure, *houri*. Now and always." Lifting Leila in his arms, he laid her in his bed and showed her with his body what his heart had just learned. Loving each other made the sex sweeter, the orgasms more intense. It made the future something to anticipate with joy instead of dread.

After they came, while Jamil held Leila he thought again about the necklace with the eye. "When you held Brian's necklace this morning. That's when I realized I loved you," he murmured against her hair.

Leila snuggled closer, her breath tickling his chest and making his cock begin to stir again. When she spoke, her voice was full of wonder. "You saw the tear go away, too, didn't you?"

Epilogue

Outside Washington, DC, six weeks later

☙

Like everything else Leila had seen during the week they'd been here in America, her private hospital room seemed larger than life—more like the luxury suite in the Kuwait City hotel where they'd spent their honeymoon than like the inside of any hospital she'd seen back home.

Each day away from his captivity, Jamil grew stronger, handsomer, more sure of himself in the way he walked and talked and presented himself to others. But he'd shown no signs that the coy glances from women on the streets drew more than his passing notice. And he'd assured her on their wedding night that he would take no other wives.

No longer the defenseless prisoner whose helplessness she'd exploited but a powerful sheikh whose wealth if not his home had survived her country's invasion years ago, Jamil still seemed content with her, scars and all. And he'd told her before they boarded the plane to come here a week ago that whether to have this surgery or not must be her decision.

Though she realized it would take more magic than even the most skilled surgeon possessed to completely restore her former looks, Leila wanted to be beautiful in her husband's eyes. She yearned to walk at his side dressed in some of the beautiful western garments she'd seen on other women, and not have strangers stare at her in horror. And she wanted the children she and Jamil would have someday, *insha'Allah*, not to recoil at the sight of her.

Leila wanted that badly enough to endure the pain Dr. d'Angelo had said would follow the first of several complex procedures he would do tomorrow morning. Idly, she reached up and stroked the uneven surface of her ruined cheek, wondered how it would feel once the skin grafts healed.

"Are you afraid, *houri*?" Jamil asked when he looked up from the English-language newspaper he'd been reading. "You don't have to put yourself through this, you know."

"I want to. I only fear the doctors won't be able to improve the scars all that much." She smiled, tightening the skin beneath her fingers. "I thank you for making this possible. I'd never expected..."

"Quiet. I had never expected to leave that prison camp alive. I do now a very small favor for you compared with the way you risked your life for me. Know, however, that I love you as you are. And I will love you always, whether or not the surgery restores your beauty as you hope it will."

He held her gaze, as though determined to convince her of what his every action had shown in the weeks since he'd been free. He loved her.

She loved him, as well. Allah could not have found her a better man than she'd picked for herself and entrapped out of pure desperation.

It struck her then that she had not told him often enough what was in her heart...and that she wanted him to know.

"Come and sit beside me," she said, patting the edge of the bed.

When he gathered her in his arms and held her, the reassuring thump-thump of his heartbeat reverberated against her ear.

Very gently Jamil stroked Leila's ruined cheek. "I want you to have this for yourself, because it means so much to you. You must know I love the beauty I see within your soul. *Insha'Allah*, the surgeons will work their magic and you will soon be able to look in a mirror and not grieve for what was taken from you."

Suddenly her anxiety went away. She wasn't afraid, couldn't fear anything with Jamil here at her side, loving her. "I love you, my husband."

She loved him enough to go through hell to become the best that she could be. Enough to believe he'd still love her even if the surgery left her worse off than before.

Leila lifted her face to his, saw the barely restrained passion in his beautiful, expressive eyes. Whatever happened, whether she looked worse than before or as beautiful as she'd been before the fire, Leila had Jamil.

And he had her.

About the Author

೩ଠ

First published in 1996, Ann Jacobs has sold more than thirty-five books and novellas. A CPA and former hospital financial manager, she now writes full-time except, of course, for the hours she devotes to being a wife and mother to seven kids. A transplanted midwesterner, she's lived in west-central Florida all her adult life.

Ann loves writing Romantica - to her, it's the perfect blend of sex, sensuality, and happily-ever-after commitment between one man and one woman.

Ann Jacobs welcomes mail from readers. You can write to her c/o Ellora's Cave Publishing at 1056 Home Avenue Akron OH 44310-3502.

Why an electronic book?

We live in the Information Age—an exciting time in the history of human civilization, in which technology rules supreme and continues to progress in leaps and bounds every minute of every day. For a multitude of reasons, more and more avid literary fans are opting to purchase e-books instead of paper books. The question from those not yet initiated into the world of electronic reading is simply: *Why?*

1. ***Price.*** An electronic title at Ellora's Cave Publishing and Cerridwen Press runs anywhere from 40% to 75% less than the cover price of the exact same title in paperback format. Why? Basic mathematics and cost. It is less expensive to publish an e-book (no paper and printing, no warehousing and shipping) than it is to publish a paperback, so the savings are passed along to the consumer.

2. ***Space.*** Running out of room in your house for your books? That is one worry you will never have with electronic books. For a low one-time c ost, you can purchase a handheld device specifically designed for e-reading. Many e-readers have large, convenient screens for viewing. Better yet, hundreds of titles can be stored within your new library—on a single microchip. There are a variety of e-readers from different manufacturers. You can also read e-books on your PC or laptop computer. (Please note that Ellora's

Cave does not endorse any specific brands. You can check our websites at www.ellorascave.com or www.cerridwenpress.com for information we make available to new consumers.)

3. *Mobility.* Because your new e-library consists of only a microchip within a small, easily transportable e-reader, your entire cache of books can be taken with you wherever you go.

4. *Personal Viewing Preferences.* Are the words you are currently reading too small? Too large? Too… ANNOYING? Paperback books cannot be modified according to personal preferences, but e-books can.

5. *Instant Gratification.* Is it the middle of the night and all the bookstores near you are closed? Are you tired of waiting days, sometimes weeks, for bookstores to ship the novels you bought? Ellora's Cave Publishing sells instantaneous downloads twenty-four hours a day, seven days a week, every day of the year. Our webstore is never closed. Our e-book delivery system is 100% automated, meaning your order is filled as soon as you pay for it.

Those are a few of the top reasons why electronic books are replacing paperbacks for many avid readers.

As always, Ellora's Cave and Cerridwen Press welcome your questions and comments. We invite you to email us at Comments@ellorascave.com or write to us directly at Ellora's Cave Publishing Inc., 1056 Home Avenue, Akron, OH 44310-3502.

THE
☥ ELLORA'S CAVE ☥
LIBRARY

Stay up to date with Ellora's Cave Titles in Print with our Quarterly Catalog.

TO RECIEVE A CATALOG,
SEND AN EMAIL WITH YOUR NAME
AND MAILING ADDRESS TO:

CATALOG@ELLORASCAVE.COM

OR SEND A LETTER OR POSTCARD
WITH YOUR MAILING ADDRESS TO:

CATALOG REQUEST
c/o ELLORA'S CAVE PUBLISHING, INC.
1056 HOME AVENUE
AKRON, OHIO 44310-3502

MAKE EACH DAY MORE *EXCITING* WITH OUR

Ellora's Cavemen Calendar

☥ www.EllorasCave.com ☥

Cerridwen, the Celtic Goddess of wisdom, was the muse who brought inspiration to storytellers and those in the creative arts. Cerridwen Press encompasses the best and most innovative stories in all genres of today's fiction. Visit our site and discover the newest titles by talented authors who still get inspired - much like the ancient storytellers did, once upon a time.

Cerridwen Press
www.cerridwenpress.com

Discover for yourself why readers can't get enough of the multiple award-winning publisher

Ellora's Cave.

Whether you prefer e-books or paperbacks,

be sure to visit EC on the web at
www.ellorascave.com

for an erotic reading experience that will leave you breathless.